CAPTIVA

A Robert Cederberg Novel

Roger C. Lubeck

CAPTIVA

CAPTIVA
It Is What It Is Press
ISBN-13: 978-0983728160
ISBN-10: 098372816X
LCCN: 2013934629
BISAC: Fiction / Suspense
211 Pages

Revised 12/15/2015
It Is What It Is Press
299 S. Foothill Blvd.
Cloverdale, California, 95425
iwiipress.com

ROBERT CEDERBERG

Robert Cederberg is a modern day Don Quixote. In Bullseye, we meet Robert Cederberg. Robert is a man with a dark past. When he was twelve, he killed a man and got away with his crime. Growing up fascinated by guns, he hung out at a seedy gun club, the Bullseye on the east side of Detroit. When Robert returned from Vietnam, the Bullseye offered him sanctuary; the tradeoff was that owning the Bullseye cost him the lives of everyone about whom he cared.

Now Robert is living on the beach on Captiva Island in Florida. One night Robert saves a young woman from drowning. In saving Nina, Robert becomes a modern day Don Quixote and his Dulcinea, Nina, turns out to be a drug addict and a prostitute desperate to escape her drug dealing boyfriend and his crew. After learning that Nina has died from an overdose at the hands of her boyfriend, Robert travels to Immokalee to investigate Nina's death. When Robert confronts Nina's boyfriend, his uncle, Don Valdez, a local drug lord warns Robert to go home and stop tilting at windmills. Days later when Robert's younger brother, mother, and father are involved in a car accident, Robert's obligations to his family and his sense of responsibility for the dead girl lead him into a violent drama carried out in the grasslands and white beaches of Southern Florida.

Dedication

To Lynette Chandler,
For those days when there is enough time.
To Bob and Doris for introducing me to
Captiva and Naples Florida.

Table of Contents

1. SWIMMING TO TEXAS   1

2. JACK'S   15

3. SAUL AND GEORGE   27

4. JUST ASKING   49

5. BLOOD TRAILS   71

6. BROTHERS   89

7. HOSPITAL VISITS   107

8. FRESH STARTS   121

9. COUNSEL   139

10. DEFENSIVE POSITIONS   163

11. LOOSE ENDS   183

12. ABOUT THE AUTHOR   199

CAPTIVA

A Robert Cederberg Novel

SWIMMING TO TEXAS
Chapter 1

Three years ago, the man who taught me everything about guns was killed in a confidence game, a romance swindle gone bad. At stake, a piece of land needed for a freeway in Detroit. Ultimately, I inherited the land, which I sold for more money than I deserved and I bought a house on Captiva beach. I moved to Florida to escape my past. Unfortunately, who you are has a way of catching up with you. My name is Robert Cederberg.

Watching the girl in the white dress sway down the beach, I assumed she was trying to walk off too many margaritas consumed at the Mucky Duck. The beach is different at midnight, the sand feels cold and moist, and the waves shimmer in the moonlight, phosphorescent foam against the black sky. Sitting on my third floor observation deck, I can see half a mile in either direction. My house is the last in a row of seven beach homes built by the Sunset Captiva Corporation in the seventies. Like the others on the beach, the house is on stilts. The bungalows set back from the water have ground floors the ocean will one day wash away. Such is life on an island.

When the girl walked past I could not see her face, but I imagined her to be in her early twenties, probably on vacation. I pictured her boyfriend passed out in the back seat of a rental car parked down the street at the Island Store. From my observation perch, I've watched thousands of midnight walks along this stretch of beach. As such, I wasn't worried when the she stepped into the water.

The water in May is still too cold for most, but everyone puts a foot in, not many swim. When she pulled off her dress, revealing bare breasts and black underwear I considered joining her. Swimming at midnight is fun if you are sober, and a little dangerous if you are not. The thing that tourists fail to realize is that forty feet off Captiva's sugar sand beaches there are bull sharks and hammerheads, man-eaters. In the ocean, things that go bump in the night are probably there to eat.

Standing in the water up to her knees, she looked back towards the shore. At this time of year, the water is still warm, but colder than the air. When the water reached her waist, she dove in breaking the surface with strong strokes, pulling hard. The moment she started swimming, I started down the two flights of stairs to the beach. I'm not sure why, but I had a feeling. The girl was swimming to Texas and she would drown long before she reached Port Isabel.

I had to stop to disengage the front door from the alarm system. My Walter PPK was sitting on the side table besides my keys. I wonder if I should take the gun. Ever since I helped put Louise Weise in jail, I've been waiting for an attack. Was this girl a ruse to draw me out of the house? Would there be someone waiting outside with a silenced pistol? Anything was possible I supposed, but I could not ignore my feeling that the girl was in trouble.

Running down the beach it took me a moment to find the girl's dress and then the girl. Picking up the dress, I stepped into the water. She was still swimming away from the beach, perhaps two hundred feet out. Too far to catch, and far enough out that the water was over her head.

"Hey you, girl!" I cupped a hand to my mouth. "You swimming, stop!"

She broke her stroke and dog paddled looking back in at the beach.

"Come in," I waved and crossed my arms. "It's dangerous. Sharks!" By now, I was standing in the water up to my waist and the girl was dog paddling some one hundred feet away. Still too far to swim to in time. Usually the threat of sharks is enough to drive visitors out of the water, even though there has never been a shark attack off this beach.

Trying to be heard over the crash of the waves, I put my hands around my mouth calling out, "You should come in. Sharks feed at night in the deeper water. Please come in. I don't want anything to happen to you."

"I don't have any clothes on," she called back.

"Here's your dress." I held out the dress without turning away. If she was intent on suicide, the moment was critical. She had to decide whether she wanted to live, and whether she could trust me. Decisions I could only help her with by standing firm. When she started in, I walked out to meet her. Walking up to me, she took the dress and pulled it over her head as if she was at Macy's on a bargain day. The wet dress clung to her body.

"Did you think I was going to kill myself?"

"It seemed possible."

"I wasn't planning to. I just love the ocean."

"I know what you mean, but it is dangerous at night. Different, unforgiving."

Walking side by side, we left the water, until we stood several feet from the water's edge. She looked around, searching the beach. Perhaps I had saved her life, but she acted as if she was still in danger.

"So what are you the unofficial life guard around here?" She asked and laughed like she was flirting.

"I'm just a guy who lives on the beach down from a bar," I answered pointing to my house. "I'm not an official anything. I just didn't want to see you hurt." Looking at her, shivering, I resisted the desire to hug her. "Can I get you something?"

"A towel would be great, if you could manage it."

"Of course. Do you want to come in or wait here?" Pointing to the path leading to my house, I couldn't take my eye off her breasts.

"Will I be intruding?" she asked.

"No, I'm alone."

"I'll come in," she said. "I'm Nina."

"I'm Robert. Robert Cederberg," I said not sure where this was headed.

"I have to get my purse," she said walking back towards the Mucky Duck. "I left it by the picnic tables," she added and I started to follow.

We were half way between my house and the Duck when something in the purposefulness of her walk gave me pause. I was unarmed, I left my house open, and she was going to reach her purse before I could make it back to the house.

Stepping off the path, I let her go on alone to the picnic tables, while I slipped back behind a tree and then faded into the darkness under a neighbor's house. Nina grabbed up her purse, reached in and pulled out a pack of cigarettes. Using a Bic lighter she lit a cigarette, inhaled deeply, and then started looking around for me.

"Robert," she called. Putting the lighter and cigarette pack back in the purse, she walked back towards the front my house calling my name as she came. From my point of view, she still had her hand in the purse, and smoking a cigarette did not make her any less dangerous. When she was out of sight, I ran back of my house and I watched as she walked and called out. When she reached my house, she started to call out again. Quietly, I came up behind her from the street side and grabbed the purse out of her hand.

"Hey, what the fuck!"

"Sorry," I said, turning the purse over, the contents falling to the sand. In the center of a pile of lipstick and Kleenex landed a .25 caliber Beretta. She made a grab for it, but I slapped her and knocked her hard onto her back. Scooping up the gun, I slipped off the safety and dragged her by the collar into the brush behind my house. Keeping the gun at my side, I whispered, "You need to tell me want is going on. Why do you have a gun, and what you are doing here? Whatever you say, do not lie."

"I told you, I was drinking at the Mucky Duck. I got high and wanted to take a swim. Maybe a last swim. When you came after me, I changed my mind."

"Are you alone?"

"I had a fight with my boyfriend, Andy.

"Where is he now?"

"I don't care, he is an asshole."

"Yeah, well, I care. So where is Andy, and why the gun?"

"He gave it to me. He's a fucking gun nut. He thinks he's Billy the Kid."

"Is he carrying?"

"They all are. Boys with big guns and little dicks! Andy and his fucking posse. We came here for a nice dinner, and then he says he wants to watch while I do his friends there on the beach."

"Apparently he's not the jealous type?"

"Are you kidding, he has beaten up guys just for talking to me, but his boys are different, he is their patron." She gave me a 'men are hopeless' look.

"Actually," she said, her tone softening, "When we are alone, he can be really sweet, but his bodyguards are assholes. Even if they paid for it, I wouldn't do them."

Learning that Nina had an armed boyfriend with bodyguards changed my perspective on the situation. I had been planning to offer her the shelter of my house, a place to sleep it off. Now, all I wanted was to get her away before there was trouble.

"I think you need to go home. Where do you live?" I asked.

"Immokalee."

"What's in Immokalee?"

"Lettuce and Mexicans."

"What are you, the farmer's daughter?"

"No, I'm a stripper, at a bar called Jack's." Stripper and prostitute, I thought. "Jack's in Immokalee," I said, trying to picture the place.

"Yes."

"Where's your car?"

"At the end of the street."

"Do you have the keys?"

"It's my car. We came in two cars."

"Okay, Nina, we are going to walk to your car." I handed her back her purse. "Find the key, follow me, and stay low. We are going to run from here to that yellow house across Sunset lane."

She looked back towards the Duck.

"Okay, are you ready?"

"Ready."

"Run to that yellow house and wait for me." I sent her running. If Andy or any of his posse were out there waiting, the Beretta and I would be there to protect her. When she reached the yellow house, I followed staying low. I kept us moving down the street, using the shadows from each house for protection. When we reached Captiva Drive, we stood back from the empty street.

"Where is your car?"

"I'm in the parking lot. It's a blue Honda, Civic," she said, pointing down the street. Nina's Honda was one of several cars parked across from the pay phone at the Royal Shell Vacations building.

"Look," I said, "I'm going to call the police. When they arrive, I'm going back to my house and look for your boyfriend. When the police show up, you should go."

"Go where?"

"Anywhere you want, but my suggestion is not back to Andy or Jack's. Get out while you have the chance."

"But, Jack owes me money. I've a job and an apartment."

"Nina, believe me, none of that matters when you are dead." She gave me a look that said I'm already dead, so I squeezed her hand.

"There is always tomorrow," I said. "Make a clean start, of it. Go now and don't look back." Seeing it was pointless to say more, I started to leave when she pulled me back in the shadows and kissed me. Her kiss was sweet and deep, frightened, but on the edge of passion. I wanted was to kiss her back, instead I ran down the block to the phone at the Royal Shell.

It took a squad car seven minutes to reach the corner across from the Island Store. When the cruiser pulled up, blue lights flashing but no siren, I ran to the car keeping my eyes on the Blue Honda in the parking lot across the street.

"Hello, Barry," I said to the officer in the passenger seat.

"Mister Cederberg, what's this about an intruder?"

"I think there may be three men with guns somewhere between the Duck and my house. They have been drinking." I explained about Nina and her boyfriend and handed Barry the Beretta. I did not mention that Nina was across the street. I made it seem like I let her go and called the police. I knew Barry understood about my past, he knew that I had dangerous enemies. Looking across the street, I saw Nina drive away in the Honda.

"You might want to call for back up," I suggested.

"Perhaps you should get in the car, and let us do our job," said the officer behind the steering wheel. His name was Noble and he made it clear he was the senior officer, and didn't need my advice.

My house was the only one with lights on. Noble said he wanted to check my house before searching the beach. Drawing his revolver, he went around to the front.

Telling me to wait, Barry Klein went up the back stairs to the screen door. Standing to the side, he knocked hard shouting. "Police." When this got no reaction, he shouted "Captiva Police," and started to open the back door into the kitchen. As he did, two shots exploded from the front of the house, followed by the sound of an automatic weapon.

"Get down!" I screamed.

Klein turned to come down the steps when his body lifted in the air collapsing in a broken pile at the foot of the steps. I checked on Klein, he was dead. Watching the back door for movement, I took Klein's revolver out of his hand.

Moving around the side of the house, I saw Officer Noble lying on the sand by the front steps. Running towards the Mucky Duck were two men carrying a third. As they passed the last house, its front light came on.

"Officer," I whispered, "Barry's dead." I hesitated, not remembering the man's name for a moment. The blood pumping out of his body onto the sand looked like a shadow in the moonlight.

"Call for help. I need an ambulance..." Before he could say more, he passed out. Turning him over, I felt his back and legs for exit wounds. He had a leg wound and a bullet in the chest. I thought about running into the house, to call for help, but I was afraid he might bleed out. From my experience in Vietnam, I worried more about the leg wound. Using my shirt, I tied off his leg and I started shouting for help.

Eventually the lights went on in the house next to mine, a rental with a family from Ohio, the father; a guy whose name was Ted or Ned opened the lanai screen door.

"Help. Call for an ambulance, we need a doctor. And, call the police." I shouted.

"I'm a doctor, what's going on?" he called from inside the porch screen.

"This is a policeman, he's been shot."

10

With this announcement, the man stuck his head back inside the house, said something, and then came running out with a small first aid kit.

"What kind of doctor are you?"

"ENT, but I worked in an ER."

"He has a leg wound and a chest wound," I said, standing up to give the doctor some room. "Is it Ted?" I asked

"Fred actually. Fred Bitter." In the distance, I heard sirens. Stepping back, I surveyed the area. Several of the houses down the beach had their porch lights on. Kneeling, next to Bitter, I watched for movement in the brush.

"Is that a gun?"

"Yes."

"Are we in danger?"

"I'll feel better when the police arrive."

I cannot say for sure how many police officers work for the city of Captiva or how many police cars the city owns, but by morning, the street behind my back yard looked like a police station. Sitting at the table on the porch, I watched as technicians took fingerprints and dug bullets out of the doors and walls, all without saying anything to me. One technician spent twenty minutes digging a line of machine gun bullets out of the front door. I could see bullet holes in the doorframe where Officer Noble had fired into the house.

One of the lanai panels was missing where a second man jumped through the screen onto the beach. My guess is he was firing the machine gun to clear his way. Thinking back on the sound of it, I guess it was probably an Uzi.

A detective named Stanley Gibson arrived and asked if I would like to talk downtown, meaning in the Captiva police station. Instead, I suggested we sit on the third floor deck, have a cup of coffee, and watch the sunrise.

The door to the third floor observation deck is through the master bedroom. On the side of the deck, there is a ladder to the roof, from which you can see completely around the island, 360 degrees. When a big storm comes in, I like to sit on the upper deck and watch it clock around the island. This morning I was satisfied to be alive and drinking coffee.

"You say the girl's name was Nina and she said she worked as a dancer at Jacks in Immokalee?"

"That's right."

"And, you've never seen her before tonight." Detective Gibson appeared to be a classic Florida cop, probably played football in high school, ex-military, fishes on weekends, and drinks too much beer at night. The only thing out of place was he wore Allen Edmond shoes and his sport coat looked Italian.

"Never seen her before."

"And, you think the men in your house were her boyfriend, this guy Andy, and his friends." Gibson sipped from his coffee. Looking out along the beach.

"She said they were his bodyguards." I added.

"Why would this Andy want to kill you? What are you to him?"

"Nothing. I think all he wanted was Nina. My guess is he was in the house because he thought she was in there with me." I could tell Gibson didn't believe me, and I didn't blame him.

"So, when Klein called out 'Police,' they tried to go out the front."

"Right, and ran into Noble."

Gibson stood and stretched. Walking to the side of the deck, he looked over the roof back towards the mainland. He and I both knew the Sanibel police should have caught Andy and his friends going over the bridge but they missed them.

"Mr. Cederberg, someone is going to pay for Klein and Noble. In my experience, even a harden criminal hesitates when it comes to shooting at the police. Yet, you say this Andy, who was in your house, presumably looking for his girlfriend, opened up when Klein knocked on the back door."

"Actually, it sounded like Officer Noble shot first and they returned fire."

"And all you know about this man is his name."

"That and he lives in Immokalee and I'm guessing he is a Mexican. I bet the Immokalee police will know who he is."

"I've already talked to the Immokalee police."

"So?"

"They are looking for a boy named Andy Valdez."

"What about the girl?"

"I'm confident we will find her." He closed his notebook, giving me a hard look. "I'm still bothered about your role in all this. Could Andy and Nina be a hit team hired to take you out?"

"If Louise Weise arranged a hit, Nina would have been a German girl carrying a silenced twenty-two. These were punk kids, Hispanics, with machine guns."

"Around here machine guns mean drugs. Are you involved in drugs, Mr. Cederberg?"

"Never use them."

"How about machine guns? Do you sell machine guns?"

"I sell the ammo, but not the guns. I've club members who own Uzis, but when they ask about using the range, I tell them our policy is no full autos. Go into the swamp if you want to shoot machine guns.

"Have you had any recent problems at your club?"

"No, business is good." There was no reason mentioning the Mexican trying to buy too much ammo or the two Indians who wanted armor piercing rounds for a hunting rifle. There was an unofficial war going on in South Florida, but this was different. Nina and her boyfriend had drawn me out my shell and now the only place to go was Immokalee.

JACK'S

Chapter 2

People arrive on Captiva before sunrise to collect shells. I spent the sunrise, trying to convince Detective Gibson that I was an innocent bystander. It took the rest of the morning working with a repairman to replace the back door and reconnect the alarm. When he finished, I set the alarm, placed the Walther by my bedside, and slept.

When I got up and saw the carnage done to the house, I felt like it was time to act. In school, kids called me "The Turtle" because I was slow and overweight. Truth is, even after losing most of the weight, as a man of thirty, I tend to play it safe, staying in my shell and watching the world go by. Last night, men I've never met, killed a policeman in my home because I tried to help a girl who was fighting with their boss. Common sense told me to leave the investigation to the police, experience told me otherwise. I decided to go to Immokalee.

At the east end of the bridge to the mainland, the police were checking every car. I knew it was stupid to be going to Immokalee, especially alone. What I should have done was go to the Club and pick up Saul Bernstein. When it came to trouble, Saul was the guy you wanted next to you. However, I wasn't looking for trouble and besides in the glove compartment, I had the Walther.

Downtown Immokalee is little more than rows of one-story cinderblock buildings, gas stations, the packing and produce center, and a thousand trailers. I stopped at a gas station to ask directions and look at a phone book. When I mentioned the town was bigger than I remembered, the attendant volunteered that the population had increased from three thousand to eleven thousand in ten years. When I asked what everyone did here, he said, "Most folks are farmers and migrant workers." Reading the signs in the gas station window, I guessed people spoke as much Spanish as English. Add to that a few blacks, some Seminole Indians, and fill in the gaps with hardscrabble Florida crackers and you had Immokalee.

According to the phone book, Jack's Bar was on New Market Road. At the third stop light, I saw Jack's on the corner. Turning down Charlotte Street I drove past the bar and turned around. Jack's Sport Bar was a three-room cinderblock building. Once painted white, the outside of the bar was peeling and had turned a sort of faded yellow, green you see in poor sections of Florida. The packed parking lot beside the bar was a collection of beat-up pickup trucks and twenty year-old station wagons, many with bumper stickers supporting the United Farm Workers. Up the road from the parking lot, the next-door neighbor had attached an above ground pool to a doublewide trailer, the good life in Immokalee.

I parked by the trailer and watched for a while. Groups of farm workers arrived and left with considerable regularity, staying for what I guessed were two beers and several dances from the advertised 'Semi naked Go-Go Dancers'.

Walking into Jack's was like entering another world. The place smelled of men's sweat, fried food, stale beer, with just a hint of manure. The tables were crowded with brown men in jeans, dirty T-shirts, and work boots. Farm workers with rough hands, unshaved weather beaten faces gave me a look that said, 'what are you doing here'? After three years in South Florida, I still dressed as if I was in living in Grosse Pointe: khaki pants, Izod shirt, and loafers. In a bar like Jack's where washed jeans and a clean shirt would have been dressed up, I stood out.

Behind the bar, an old white man leaned on the counter reading a newspaper. He was wearing a stained white apron with a wash and wear white dress short-sleeved shirt underneath. He looked to be in his late sixties or early seventies. His clothes and stubble beard said classic Florida Cracker, but he had high cheekbones, dark eyebrows and black eyes suggested he might be part Indian.

"What time are the dancers," I asked, putting a foot on a bar stool.

"6:00 o'clock on the weekends. Today's Monday, no dancers. Tonight is taco night."

"What night isn't?" I asked.

The old man laughed and gave me a considered look.

"Friday is fish night," he said. "We offer fish on Fridays for the Catholics." He walked over and set the towel on the counter in front of me. "What can I get you?"

"How about a Bud." I said, sitting down on a cracked red leather stool.

"Bud it is." The old man walked off to a cooler and returned with an open long neck Budweiser. He wiped the counter and set the beer in front of me.

Drinking the beer, I enjoyed the coldness, but the bitter aftertaste reminded me why I stopped drinking Budweiser.

"You a cop?" asked the old man.

"No. Far from it." I smiled and drank another sip of Bud. A jukebox in the corner was playing Merle Haggard's 'Barroom Buddies'.

"You're not from Immokalee."

"No. I live on the gulf."

"What are you doing here?"

"I'm looking for a girl named Nina. She said she worked here as a dancer. Do you know her?"

"We have lots of dancers come through here."

"Dark short hair, in her early twenties. Good looking."

"To me, they're all good looking."

"Look, I don't want trouble. I'm not a cop. I met a girl named Nina, who said she worked here. Do you know where I can reach her?"

I put two twenties on the counter.

"Is she in trouble?"

"She could be, but not from me. I only met her last night."

"So, why you are looking for this Nina?"

18

"Last night she tried to drown herself and I stopped her. She was with her boyfriend. Some guy named Andy. She said he had bodyguards. I helped her escape. When I went home, the boyfriend was waiting."

"Wait, are you the guy with the house that was all shot up on Captiva. I read about you in the paper. Says a cop was shot." The old man got the paper and returned.

"Killed by someone with a machine gun," I said.

"And Nina was involved, but the police let her go?"

"No, I let her go. I called the police and let her go before they came. I told her to run, because I was afraid her boyfriend might not understand. Turns out he and his boys were waiting in my house. So what can you tell me about Nina or this guy Andy?"

"Nina does work for me, but, let's start with Andy. Andy Valdez. He and Nina were in school together. Both were wild kids, hippies. They dated in high school, but Andy went away for college. He got good grades and his uncle is rich. He told Nina he was going places, and then his dad died, and Andy came back to Immokalee. He and Nina took up where they left off, only now they're junkies. First, it was heroin, now its cocaine. They were living together at one time over the laundry on Post. Then, Andy went in for the treatment and she tells me they are finished. Trouble is, he is always hanging around when she is dancing. Fighting with customers. What was Nina doing on Captiva?" he asked.

"She and this Andy were drinking at a local bar on the beach, the Mucky Duck."

"I know that place. I take my grandkids to the Bubble room."

"How about Nina, did you see her today?"

"No, I honestly ain't seen her."

"Would you tell me if you did?"

"I might, I just can't figure what's she to you? Why is she so important, that you come looking."

"I just want to find her. Make sure she is safe."

"Who are you? The paper didn't mention your name."

"My name is Cederberg."

"The paper said the shooting at your house was a robbery gone bad. Was this a drug deal?"

"No, I told you. I was afraid she might kill herself. I thought she was a girl who needed help."

"She is. I've known Nina since she was a baby. Her mother drank herself to death. Nina went into foster care as an infant. Later the tribe took her in and instructed her in the Seminole ways."

"Are you related?"

"We all are if you go back far enough. Nina' mother was my second cousin. For a time, Nina lived with my family when she was in high school. I hoped she would marry within the tribe, but instead…"

"Instead, she's a go-go dancer at your bar! If you cared so much about her, why let her work here as a…"

"Go ahead, you can say it. I know what she is. The thing is, when you love someone, you do foolish things. Nina started working here as a waitress. I gave her a job to help her after high school. One

20

night she was out there dancing. She made good money and begged me to let her dance. Eventually, she started going off with men, after work. Then Andy returned, and everything went to hell. Nina wants to be a good person; it's just Andy and the drugs."

"Is there someplace Nina might be hiding?   Could she be at her apartment?   Someplace on the reservation?"

"She's not in town. The police are looking for her."

"What about Andy?"

"I heard the cops talked to him this morning. Apparently several witnesses place Andy in Ft. Myers at the time of the shooting." The old man looked at his newspaper for a moment.

 "Last night, were any of your intruders shot?   The paper didn't say."

"I think one man might have been. Did you hear something?"

"Tom Burton one of the deputy sheriffs came around looking for Nina. He asked if I had heard about anyone being shot."

"Had you?"

"At the time, no, but right before you came in, a couple of boys who work for Frank Valdez asked if I knew a doctor who made house calls. They said Boca needed a doctor. Boca is Andy' shadow. Tough guy. Dangerous and unpredictable. Carries a gun and a knife."

"Maybe you should mention that to Sheriff Tom."

"Or, you could mention it to the Captiva police, just as easy."

"Seems like neither of us likes talking to police."

"You're an interesting fellow. What did you say your name was?

"Cederberg, Robert."

"Jack Jensen," he said, offering his hand. It was as hard as he was.

"What do you do Robert?"

"I own a gun club in Ft Myers."

"The new one on the beach?" he asked.

"Yes."

"That's a nice looking place. I seen it driving to the mall. You took the bars off the windows. You're either awful trusting or have very good connections." Jensen touched his finger to his nose.

"No, just security glass. Next time you are by, you should stop in." I handed the old man my card.

"Can I ask you a professional question?"

"Sure."

"What kind of gun would you recommend; for the bar I mean?"

"Smith and Wesson .38 cal. police special is a great gun. If you are interested, I can give you a very good deal on a used snub nose."

"You think a.38 has enough stopping power?"

"In a bar, you want a big gun, one that is accurate but with real stopping power. You want the bad guy to see it and stop what he is doing. The Colt .45 is a great gun, real stopping power, but it only has seven shots. The .44 magnum is impressive too, but heavy

22

and only six shots. Some of the new autos from Europe have clips with nine or fifteen shots." The old man opened several beers and handed them to a waitress who had been waiting at the counter. She was older and showed too much cleavage, not that the farmers were complaining, I'd guess. I wondered if I should try to talk with her about Nina.

"What about a shotgun?" he asked.

"You would need a sawed off gun. My guess is you already know they are illegal in Florida. However, if you find an old sawed off for sale, it can be restored.

"What would you buy, if you was me?"

"I'm a pistol man, but in Vietnam I carried a Winchester. It is longer, but you have more rounds." I laid five dollars on the bar. "If you want to look at guns, or if you hear from Nina, give me a call at my Club. If I'm not there and you want to talk about a gun, ask for George. He is the Club's salesman. If you are calling with information about Nina, ask for Saul and leave a message."

"What does Saul do?"

"He's my problem solver."

"And, what about you, Robert? What are you, the money man; the silent partner who lives on the beach?"

"If I was I wouldn't be here. I'm the shooter. Every club has to have a shooter and I'm him."

"Do you compete? Shooting at little paper targets?"

"I use to be a competitive shooter, but instructing keeps me fairly busy."

"Perhaps, I should arrange something out here where you could do some real shooting."

"Just call if you hear from Nina."

"What are you going to do now?"

"I'm going to check for Nina at her apartment on Post Street."

"It's the rental over the pay laundry. Like I said, I looked for her this afternoon. She ain't there."

"Could she be with Andy?" I asked.

"Robert, can I give you some advice?"

"Sure."

"I like you. I appreciate that you saved Nina from herself and Andy. You have done enough. You need to leave this alone. Go back to your club and your house on the beach. Nina is family, and I love her, but she is trouble and so is Andy. He is a punk kid with a dead father and a powerful uncle. Frank Valdez owns the biggest farm in the county. He owns the Produce Center. He drives a Mercedes and has a private airplane. He does business in Mexico and Columbia. He is no one to mess with." The old man threw his bar towel down on the bar.

"If Nina comes in, will you give her my card?"

"I'm not sure."

"If you hear she is safe, will you at least call me?"

"I might, if you'll tell me why you are so interested in Nina? What is she to you? I mean, she is pretty and all, but she is trouble."

"I'm not sure. I guess I hate loose ends. Last night, I think she would have killed herself if I had not stopped her. She needed someone to care about her, someone to protect her from Andy and his kind. Instead, I sent her back into the wind. Now she's a loose end." I picked up my change and thanked the old man for his time.

Before leaving town, I drove by Nina's apartment on Post Street. There were three mailboxes on the door next to the laundry. In the apartments above, the windows were dark, so I drove back to Ft. Myers, back to the Bullseye II.

SAUL AND GEORGE

Chapter 3

Monday nights in May were Police Night; cops using the range got a discount and we stayed open until 9:00 p.m. Police cruisers and trucks with gun racks and oversized mud tires filled the Bullseye II's parking lot. Looking at the crowded parking lot and the clean modern exterior of the Club, I felt pleased with what I had accomplished.

The original club in Detroit looked run down even with a new coat of paint. In renovating the building on Ft. Myers Beach, the walls were given a double coat of fresh white paint and the iron bars on the windows were removed after replacing the glass with security glass. I wanted the new club to look modern and appealing.

Pushing open the front door, I waved at Saul behind the counter in the lobby. Saul was the first employee I hired after purchasing the building. I met Saul Bernstein in the Green Parrot Bar in Key West.

According to a plaque behind the bar, the Green Parrot began as a local grocery. In World War II, the grocery became the Brown Derby Bar, a dive for submariners. When the Navy left Key West, the town became a haven for those who had dropped out, those in search of a different America. Seeing that Key West was changing, the owner, changed the Brown Derby into a spot for the local beatniks and later hippies. In the process, the bar became the Green Parrot.

It was 1978 and I was waiting for my house to be finished on Captiva, so I drove down to the Keys where I spent five days driving from one great fishing spot to another through Key Largo of Bogart fame, Marathon Key, and on to the Southernmost point in the United States.

In Key West, I tried snorkeling on a dive boat, ate cold shrimp and conch for lunch, and drank beer at Sloppy Joes. On my second night, I walked away from the tourist end of the island and wandered into the Green Parrot, a bar with live music, hot looking woman, and ice-cold beer. I was sitting at the bar, listening to a duo who were trying to imitate America. Next to me, the guy at the bar was drinking a dark beer. In Michigan, we drank bock beer in the spring. In Vietnam, dark beer like Lowenbrau was a rare treat when compared to the watered down beer provided by the Army, so I asked the guy, "What beer is that?"

"Dos Equis."

"Is it good?" I asked.

"No, asshole, I drink it because it's shit."

"Look," I said, putting up my hands. "I was just curious."

"Okay, but one answer question."

"Shoot."

"Are you queer?"

"What?"

"I come here to drink the beer and dance with chicks. I'm not interested in a boyfriend, and if that is your scene I suggest you find a different stool or a different bar."

"Are you asking if I'm a homo?"

"You look like one."

"What the fuck are you talking about?"

"Who wears khakis and a button down shirt in Florida?"

"I'm from Michigan."

Yea, well you look like a fucking Beach Boy, Brian, and I want you to move." He got down off his stool, steadying himself on the bar. He was half a foot taller than I was, but I was heavier. He had on a Grateful Dead headband, cut off blue jeans, and a tie-dyed T-shirt. He wore sandals that looked like they had been made of Goodyear tires. Later I learned they were Kino's and made in a shop two blocks from the real Sloppy Joes. At the time, all I remember thinking was this guy looks like a hippie, all love and peace, but I knew a killer when I met one.

"Look, I know you are tough, and I can see you are ready to fight, but that Brian Wilson crack was pretty funny, and I don't meet many people with a sense of humor."

"So."

"So, if you want to fight, okay, but I should warn you I'm carrying, and I never fight fair."

"That makes two of us."

"I knew it. How about instead of fighting, you let me buy you another beer," I pulled out a crumpled five and handed it to the woman behind the bar. "Which service were you in?" I asked.

"Army, 25th Infantry."

"I was in the 101st."

"Vietnam."

"For a time."

"Brothers in fucking arms. This calls for Tequila." He signaled to the bartender.

"I'm Robert," I said, putting more money on the bar.

"Saul," he said, offering me a shot of tequila and a lime wedge.

"What do you think about those two at the bar, Saul?" I pointed to a pair of heavily made up girls.

"Those two are going to cost you. They are working for that guy at the end of the bar."

"How can you tell?"

"I was a bodyguard once. I'm always watching. Always on the lookout for bad guys. I saw you were carrying when you came in."

"How about the girls?"

"Actually, I fucked the smaller one two nights ago. She cost me twenty five bucks." He laughed and I joined in.

"Saul you seem like an excellent companion for a guy like me. I could use a wingman and you look like you could use a job."

"Sorry, but I gave up the protection business."

30

"What happened?"

"It is a long story," he said setting down his beer.

Two days later, with one or two exceptions, we had no secrets left to tell. Saul was on the run. He had been working in Brooklyn as an enforcer for Roscoe Geonellia a local drug dealer, when a deal turned into a robbery. Saul admitted he was slow reading the situation when the buyers showed up with extra muscle. He had a habit and was high at the time. When two of the buyers' men pulled out machine guns, Roscoe put up his hand as if to say I surrender or I give up, however, his eyes told Saul to kill these motherfuckers, which Saul tried to do. The four robbers died in an exchange of gunfire, but not before Joey Blue, Roscoe's other bodyguard was dead, and Saul and Roscoe were shot.

Saul drove Roscoe to the nearest hospital and leaving him in the emergency entrance, he ran. Fortunately, Roscoe lived and the drugs were recovered, but Saul knew Roscoe would never trust him, and eventually he would have Saul killed. For Saul Bernstein, the gunfight in Brooklyn that morning ended his life of crime in New York.

When I asked Saul if he ever worried that they would come after him, he told me, "I take life one day at a time. I fish and work odd jobs." That was when I mentioned I was opening a gun club and I asked if he would be interested in working for me. At first, he thought the idea was stupid, and then he tried to convince me living in Key West would be more fun. Eventually I made it clear I was serious and I would not take 'no' for an answer. A day later, when I left Key West, I gave him enough money to take the bus to Ft. Myers. Two months later, he arrived, broke and looking like he needed a week in a detox unit. That was a year ago.

~*~

Walking by my office, I saw my other employee George Tanner talking to Cal Fraser. Cal was a sergeant with the county Sheriff's Department. He was a big man with even bigger ambition.

"Howdy, Cal, I said, patting the cop on the back. How was the spread tonight," I asked.

"Actually, I'm here to see how you are doing. I heard about the men waiting for you at your house. What's going on?"

"Honestly Cal, I don't know what's going on. I explained about Nina and how I had gone to Immokalee this afternoon to see if she was okay."

"Did you find her?"

"No, she's flown. She was a stripper at a local bar. The bar owner's an old guy, Jack Jensen."

"I know Jack, what did he have to say?"

"He mentioned a local player named Frank Valdez. I think his nephew Andy is involved with this Nina. I'm sure he was one of the men at my house."

"So rather than leave this to the police, you went to Immokalee."

"I don't like armed men in my house. Barry Klein was a friend of mine. "

"Yeah, and now he is dead because of you. What about Saul or George, are they involved? Perhaps Saul has been buying on credit and they were there to collect."

"If they were, I would have taken care of it. Besides, Saul is clean and sober. George, do you know what is going on?" I asked for Fraser's benefit.

"Saul and I know nothing about nothing. Talk to Saul if you don't believe me," said George talking to Fraser.

"I already talked to him. Now I'm going to give you some advice." He gave me a hard look. "Stop acting like Sam Spade. Stop asking questions and definitely stay out of Immokalee. Those are bad men and if you want to keep your business license, you will refrain from any associations. If you get my meaning." The big Sergeant pulled up his black leather belt and walked out of the club.

"Asshole," said George under his breath. Like Saul, George had no love for cops.

"He is just doing his job. Don't forget Brian Klein died last night trying to protect my ass. I want to help the police find his killer."

"That doesn't mean I have to like cops."

"No, but you might not mention it on Monday night!"

"Sure," he said, closing the office door.

"How did we do today?"

"Not bad. Let me get the books."

~*~

The Bullseye II is smaller than the first club in Detroit because it has fewer ranges and the ranges are all indoors. In the front lobby, there are two long glass front counters with three shelves full of pistols for rent and sale. Against one wall are rifles. Ammunition and shooting accessories are in another counter and on display. An unmarked door leads to the member's locker room and to four ranges. Down a hall past, the door to the ranges is the only restroom, followed by my office. In the very back is a workshop. The new club makes better use of space and is a better arrangement for selling firearms and renting guns for the range. It is not a club where ex-cops hang out playing cards. It is a place where businessmen can shoot a gun at lunch. Had I understood the area and the market better at the time, I might have located downtown, but Fowlers was already established, and I wanted to be close to Captiva. As it is, the store made money because of George.

George Tanner is a year older than Saul and six years older than I am. He was born during World War II, when his father was fighting on Iwo Jima. When it came his time, George served in the Marines before Vietnam. Had he fought, I'm certain he would have received a medal for saving his platoon by falling on a grenade. George was that kind of guy, selfless and unafraid. Like Saul and me, he was a gun nut and competition shooter from childhood. In addition, George is the friendliest, nicest person anyone could meet. Club members love talking guns with George. He knows the history of every gun, and he knows which gun is right for each shooter.

George grew up in southern Alabama and went to college for one year in Tallahassee. At which point he joined the Marines. At the time, George was a classic Marine recruit, five feet ten inches, rock hard athlete, and an expert with a rifle before joining. After basic, George went to Sniper school and then the Marines, in their wisdom sent George to San Diego, where he served out his tour guarding aircraft carriers and submarines until the day his motorcycle hit a car and he hit a tree. By all reports, the brain injury George experienced was mild, affecting only his eye-hand coordination and fine motor movements. For George, serving as a sniper was out, as was competing in Ohio at the Bullseye competition.

After his discharge, George returned to Tallahassee where he took classes in business and accounting. Restless, he left school before graduating and worked in a series of gun stores selling guns and doing the books. George was a natural low-pressure salesman. He created the need in a customer and then walked away. Today, George still rides a motorcycle, only now he wears a helmet, and when he fires a gun, he aims for the largest part of the target.

I met George at Fowlers in downtown Ft. Meyers. I went into Fowlers to purchase ammunition. George was working the counter. Before I left the store, I had Georges' promise that he would have lunch with me to talk with me about designing the Bullseye II. Two days later, after lunch, he gave his notice and became a minority partner; owning twenty-five percent of the Club.

~*~

George and I reviewed the accounts and the schedule for the ranges for the rest of the week. When we finished, we talked about the men at my house and Nina. In his quiet way, George asked why I went to Immokalee, and why I went alone.

"What would Helen say," I asked George, "if I had called at five in the morning and asked you to drive to Immokalee to back me up?" Helen was George's live in girlfriend of ten years. Helen and George did not believe in marriage or religion. They believed in each other. Helen was a special education teacher.

"Helen appreciates our friendship. She would have understood."

"Truthfully, I don't know what's going on with this girl, and until I do, I'm going to avoid getting you or Saul in something that has nothing to do with you. You and I made a deal. You get the Club and take care of Saul if I'm killed. Getting you killed isn't a part of the deal."

"What about Saul? Why didn't you call him?"

"I thought about it, but I'm keeping Saul as my hole card just in case."

"Well, if you need to draw another card, you know I'm here for you." At that moment, Saul came into the office carrying a broom.

"I heard you had some trouble," he said, setting his broom aside, and giving me a bear hug.

"Yes, quite a bit."

"Was it…"

36

"No, these were men with machine guns. Any chance they were looking for you?"

"Did Fraser ask you to ask?"

"No, I'm asking. I'm the one with a dead cop in my house."

"This has nothing to do with me. I'm clean."

"What do you know about a guy in Immokalee named Valdez?"

"He is the real deal. Brings drugs into Immokalee and the Everglades every week. Rumor has it he has a factory for cutting and packaging somewhere in the glades. What's his connection to you?"

"The girl last night, Nina worked at Jack's, and Jack said she was involved with Valdez's nephew."

"Whoa, slow down partner. What girl? Jack who?"

I explained about Nina and going to Immokalee. When I finished, Saul was frowning.

"Robert, I thought we had a deal," said Saul. He looked at George for agreement. "We watch your back, and you keep us employed. What on earth did you go to Immokalee for without me?"

"Hindsight is twenty-twenty Saul, besides, if you had seen Nina, you would understand why I went alone."

"So what now?"

"I'm going to arm myself and wait."

"You want me to ask around?" Saul's eyes seemed to darken. The killer in him wanted to be released.

"Not until we are sure who they are. And, then we'll see."

~*~

For a week, I noticed more police and sheriff's cars patrolling around my house. I was certain Saul was guarding the house one night, and I saw George walk by on the beach several times that week. At the Club, nothing was said except, how are you and what are you doing tonight? After a week, we settled back into our familiar pattern. George worked the counter advising Club Members and selling guns. Saul repaired guns and took care of the ranges. I gave lessons and practiced combat shooting more than usual.

I was working in the back and Saul was at the counters on Friday morning when Jack Jenson walked in. To hear Saul tell it the old man spoke with him like they were two Miami Jews, talking in Yiddish for several minutes before Saul buzzed for me to come to the lobby.

At the counter, Jack Jenson looked like he was coming from church. White cotton dress shirt, suit pants, and black shiny shoes. He was alone, but he kept looking out the front window. When I asked, he said his wife and grandkids were waiting in the car. They were going to the Bubble Room on Captiva for lunch.

"Mister Jensen says he is interested in a shotgun." Saul said, holding out a Winchester Pump.

"Jack, it is good to see you. Have you seen Nina?"

The old man gave me a sad look and tears formed in his eyes. He played with his hat for a moment.

"I assumed you knew. The Immokalee police found her in her apartment."

"Dead?"

"Overdose. I knew the drugs would kill her."

"I'm sorry to hear that. What happened?"

"The day after I seen you, she showed up asking for money. I told her the police were looking for her. She said she planned to leave Andy. Maybe an hour later that cop I mentioned, Tom Burton shows up looking for Nina. I told him she might be at her apartment. Apparently, he found her overdosed and took her to the hospital. But, it was too late."

"Did you ever find out why she was at my house?" I asked.

"Some folks attract trouble. I think you are one of those people Mister Cederberg. Nina was damaged goods. She was looking for a way out. She was looking for someone to save her, and you were looking for someone to save. Your paths crossed you know, like they say, ships in the night."

"Are you saying it was an accident?"

"Chance brought you together. If you leave it alone, I think the interested parties in Immokalee will consider it over."

"It still feels like there are loose ends. Who pays for Nina or Barry Klein?" For a moment, I thought about Nina swimming to Texas. In hindsight, I should have let her try. Now she was dead, and I was no closer to understanding why she meant so much to me.

"Let the mayors and chiefs of police worry about the dead. You worry about the living." Jensen picked up the Winchester and squinted along the barrel.

"What do you think about this gun?" asked Jensen. He handed me the shotgun.

"Jack," I said, putting the Winchester down on the counter. "I think you need something more old school." Going to the shotgun display, I took down an Ithaca side by side. Then just to push the old man's buttons, I took down a beautiful hand engraved Fabarm. In front of him, I placed the three guns ranging in price from three hundred dollars to three thousand.

"I find that the caliber of a man is determined by his appreciation of craftsmanship and beauty. If you need a gun to stop a riot, I would consider the Ithaca. If you want a gun for hunting, a gun that no one else owns right now then I'd go with the Fabarm. Unfortunately, I don't have any English guns, they are the best, but this Fabarm is a beauty."

"In Vietnam," said Saul, "I carried a Winchester. Today, I really like the Mossberg 500."

"What do you own?" Jack asked me.

"I don't own a shotgun," I said. "I don't hunt."

"Why not?"

"I love guns, but I'm tired of killing." I gave the old cracker my 'I'm not kidding, look.' By this time, Saul was standing by my side holding up the Winchester.

"So which do you recommend?" he asked me.

"The Ithaca," I said.

"Very reliable," Saul added.

"If I buy the Ithaca, can you cut it down for me?"

"No, we cannot and we will not." I said.

"However," said Saul, "if you call this number and mention me, they will help you find a short barreled Ithaca made in the 1920s. Saul handed the old man a slip of paper that I assumed had his number on it. He had many connections in the used gun and antique gun trade.

"Call after your lunch today, after three," said Saul.

"Fair enough. I will." The old man started to leave. "Robert, about Nina. We both tried, but in the end, she made her bed."

"Thanks," I said, knowing it was never that simple.

~*~

A week later, Saul, informed me that Jack Jensen had been talking to him and he wanted the three of us to visit his gun range. It was a Tuesday morning with no appointments, so we put the sign on the door, and the three of us drove out to Immokalee in Saul's truck. When I asked about guns, Saul said, "Everything is in the tool chest in the back of the truck."

It was twelve fifteen when we arrived at Jack's bar. The old man was waiting outside sitting on the bed of a Ford F150; with him were a tall boy of fifteen or sixteen and a taller man of forty. They both wore jeans and T-shirts and looked like father and son. Hopping off the truck bed, the old man approached shaking each of our hands.

"This is my son Harry and his boy Jefferson. I asked them along to learn about the new guns."

"Guns," I said, looking at Saul.

"Robert, George and I talked to Mister Jenson about several other guns. I suggested we test them where no one would hear us."

I've never known Saul to lie or deceive me. If this made sense to him, I was willing to trust him.

Saying 'follow me,' Harry and Jack Jensen climbed into the Ford while the boy jumped into the truck's bed. We drove southeast for half an hour or so, until we pulled off on a dirt road. We were at the edge of the Everglades. The boy jumped out of the truck and unlocked the gate on a tumbled down fence. Passing through the fence, we drove another twenty minutes into the saw grass wetlands. Saul played the radio the entire way, singing along to the oldies station in Naples. When we stopped, we were in a clearing with a real Seminole Chickee hut.

"What's this?" I asked Jack.

"Indian land. My mother was a pure Seminole. This is part of the tribe's land. Sometimes the old men hold meetings out here or just sit under the Chickee and tell stories. It doesn't look like much, but we love these wetlands."

We walked about the clearing, while Harry and Jefferson unloaded a cooler of water and beer and Saul and George unloaded several gun cases from the truck tool chest. One case was obviously the Ithaca, but I was surprised to see two pistol cases and a second rifle case made out of hand tooled leather with silver clasps.

Kneeling, Saul spread out a blanket and then opened each gun case and removed the weapon. From an army backpack, he removed boxes of ammunition and five pairs of shooting glasses.

Placing the appropriate ammunition by each gun, he handed each of us a pair of glasses. On the blanket, he had Ithaca along with a snub-barreled Police .38, a .44 magnum, and a Fabarm Classic 12 Gauge shotgun. Removing a worn gun case from the Ford, Harry added an old bolt action Remington 700 with a scope. When I saw the Remington, I knew why George was there.

"Are you planning to start a war Mister Jenson?"

"No, but I might have to end a war."

"Care to explain?"

"At one time, all of this land was Indian land. The Seminole and the Miccosukee. We lived off the land, but we were a part of the land. Then the white man came with his black slaves. He farmed the land, and he too became a part of the land. Then the northern whites came. Your people came and developed the land for tourism, and now the Mexicans, Puerto Ricans, Cubans, and Colombians come to work in the jobs the whites and blacks will no longer do. Jobs that exploit more land. As Jack spoke, I began to see the Indian in him and his son and grandson. I could tell he was proud of being a Seminole."

"So why the guns, Mister Jenson?"

"Because someone has to do something about the drug dealers and criminals who have taken over Immokalee."

"Are you a vigilante?"

"No, but I plan to protect myself and my own."

"With these?" I asked, pointing to the blanket.

"If necessary."

43

"I picked up the Fabarm and looked at Saul.

"Mister Jenson called and asked me if we could make him a package deal."

"What about the Ithaca?"

"Purchased as an antique, which is how the gun is described, in the Bill of Sale. George and I made sure it is in working order."

"Have you fired it?"

"Of course. The Ithaca is like new.

"Mister Jenson, this Fabarm is a beautiful gun, I'm envious."

"Come on Robert, call me Jack."

"Okay, Jack, how would it be if we made sure you know how to use them? Let's start with pistols and then you can compare them with the two shotguns."

"So Robert, are we kosher?" Jack smiled at Saul.

"Of course, your gun is an antique, legal. I see nothing wrong with hiring someone to modify a gun you own, provided I'm not directly involved. Likewise, if you buy an antique and want to risk firing it, I say live and let live. As far as I'm concerned, I'm here to provide instruction to a good customer, and I hope a friend." I added sticking out my hand for Jack to shake.

"What do you say Saul?" Saul looked between the two of us. Turning to George, he said, "I think it is time to bring out the real fire power." George went to the truck and pulled out another blanket roll.

"Gentlemen," he said, bowing, "The AR-15 or as the Army calls it: the M-16."

44

"You have an M-16," said Harry.

"Well, technically it is an AR-15 because it can only be fired as a single shot or semi-automatic. In Vietnam, we used to curse the M-16, but now it seems like a great rifle."

"What next Saul," I asked, "a Kalashnikov?"

"That would be sweet," said George taking the unloaded M-16 and handing it to Harry.

"Be my guest," said George. "This is a great gun, and with a scope, it is a better hunting rifle than your Remington. Lighter anyway."

While George and Saul taught Harry and Jefferson how to use the M-16, I sat with Jack Jenson. He was trying to decide about the two pistols. The more I looked at the old man the more Indian he became. When the moment was right, I asked him to tell me again about Nina.

"Like I told you. She overdosed. The sheriff said the needle was still in her arm."

"Who found her, Andy Valdez?"

"No, I told you, Tom Burton; Officer Burton found her. He called an ambulance, but it was too late."

"Any evidence she had been beaten or forced?"

"I don't know. I never saw the body, but if Tom Burton thought it was a murder, I think he would have said so. Tom had a thing for Nina; they dated in high school."

"Was there a funeral or anything?"

"No, the police are still holding the body."

"Then the case isn't closed."

"Eventually we will bury her out here in the Seminole way."

"When you do, will you call me?"

"Why?"

"I know it is foolish, but I thought I saved her. Perhaps she was destined to die, and I only delayed the inevitable. I just need to close the circle."

"You sound like an Indian. Personally, I do not believe in destiny. Our future is unwritten. We make our own fate. You think that girl wanted to die because she took a late night swim to escape her asshole boyfriend. When she came back, she told me she was getting out. She said life had given her another chance. You gave her another chance. She asked for the money I owed her and when I said I would give her the money only if it would stay out of her arm, she said she was through. She promised me she was free, and I believed her."

"So what happened?"

"Maybe Andy found her; maybe one of his boys fixed her up. Maybe with three hundred dollars in her pocket, her habit took charge and destiny took over. Who can say? Two days after you and I talked in the bar, she was dead and Andy Valdez had an iron clad alibi."

On the drive home, when I mentioned Nina. Saul got a funny look, and said, "I think you should drop your fascination with this girl. She is dead and you need to move on."

"I know. It is just that she told Jack that I saved her, but I didn't, I sent her into the wind."

"What could you have done?"

"Turn her over to the cops. Make them responsible."

"No one is responsible except Nina," said George.

"And, her killer."

"You don't know she was murdered. She overdosed. There is no way to know for sure what happened."

"No, but the case is still open."

"So what's next, Bro?"

"I'd like to see Nina's apartment. Maybe talk to Andy Valdez; maybe pay a call on his uncle," I said.

"No time like the present," said Saul, giving me his before a fight look. Smiling at Saul and me, George began humming the Beatles tune: Maxwell's Hammer.

JUST ASKING
Chapter 4

Nina's apartment on Post Street was above a coin laundry. Walking up the narrow flight of steps, I had the feeling my foot might break through a step at any moment. At the top of the stairs were two doors, one painted lime green marked 22; the other painted orange, marked 21. Knocking on the green door, I smelled the perfume and marihuana before a woman in her early forties open the door.

"What do you want?" she demanded, giving me the twice over. I was glad Saul had waited in the truck. She was wearing extra wide bell-bottom jeans and a peasant blouse. There were rings on every finger, and she was smoking an unfiltered Camel cigarette. Perfect for Saul, he would have moved in.

"I'm looking for Nina." I said acting like I was an old friend or maybe a john.

"She's doesn't live here anymore. She's gone."

"Do you know where I can find her? It's rather important. She has some money coming to her." I stepped back as if to leave.

"I'm Misses Hernandez," she said, grabbing my shirt. "Estelle Hernandez. Her landlady. If she has money coming to her, perhaps you can leave it with me. Nina owed me considerable back rent. I could take out what she owes and give her the rest when she returns."

"When do you expect her soon; perhaps I should wait."

"No, she might be days."

"Or a lifetime!" I said, giving her my hard look.

"Fuck you. If you knew she was dead, why knock on my door, and ask for her. What are you another cop?"

"No, I was a friend. I just wanted to see where she lived. When I learned she had died, I wanted to see where. Could you let me see her apartment, I'll only be a minute."

"Did she take something from you is that it? Were you one of her boyfriends?" she asked ending with a throaty laugh that turned into a smokers cough. "Nina was always coming home with some new trinket from a man. Occasionally one of them shows up looking for his trinket. "

"Can I see her room?" Listening to myself, I sounded like I needed the key to the washroom. Anxious.

"Sure, all you have to do is pay her back rent, and you can have the room." She stood her ground with her palm turned up. I turned and started down the stairs.

"Wait," she called. "Give me a twenty and you can look all you want. For forty you can take a trinket of your own." She laughed when I turned back. She knew she had me and the negotiation phase was over. I handed her a twenty.

"No trinkets?" she laughed.

"If I find anything I want, I'll pay on my way out." I offered.

The room was much as I expected; clothes everywhere, unmade bed, sink with dishes, and no food in the refrigerator. She had a small black and white television from Sears with separate rabbit

50

ears on a card table by the bed. There were two folding chairs facing the television. Surprisingly, the bathroom was clean with makeup and lipsticks arranged on a shelf above the toilet. In the mirrored medicine chest, there were the usual bottles of aspirin and cold medicine. One prescription from a Dr. Nunes was for sleep problems and second for drowsiness. Junkies always needed uppers and downers, and Nina had a Doctor supplying hers. On the sink was a half completed ring of birth control. In the bathtub, she had erected some type of clothes drying apparatus. Hanging on the racks was a line of black underwear. For a moment, I considered taking a pair as my twenty-dollar souvenir. Exiting the bathroom, I was startled to find Misses Hernandez waiting.

"Seeing anything you like?"

"No. Where did they find her, I mean, where did she die?"

"On the floor in the bathroom. He found her on the floor."

"Who do you mean? Who found her?"

"That cop found her. Tom Burton. He had been asking about her. When he came asking again, I told him I thought she was home because I heard a big fight that morning."

"Was Andy here?"

"No, it was that other guy, Andy's friend, the one with the scar. I guess the door was open, because the cop walked in and found her. Needle in her arm, foam coming out her mouth."

"There was foam coming out of her mouth. She was still alive?"

"I assume so; he carried her out to his patrol car and drove off. Next thing I heard she was dead."

"Who told you?"

"The cop. He came back looking for evidence."

"Just the cop who found her? And no finger prints guys."

"No, just him. How did you know?"

"Nothing on the walls. No black power"

"Did you find a souvenir?"

"I did," I said, handing her another twenty. "I'd like to take this picture of Nina if that is alright with you." There were a series of pictures of Nina in skimpy outfits posed as a dancer. However, among them, was one other, perhaps taken by her parents, after breakfast on Sunday morning. She was dressed in a simple black dress, much as I remembered her. "I'd like this," I said pointing to the picture.

"Take them all if you wish."

"No this one will do. Oh, and one other thing."

"Sure."

"Jack Jensen said her stage name was Nina Grace. Did she go by any other name?"

"Boy you are smitten. Paying for keepsakes and you don't even know her name. Her real name was Tiger. Nina Mae Tiger. She was part Indian. Not enough to be in the tribe I guess, but some say her real father is one-half Seminole.

"Who is her father?"

"No one is sure; she was taken away from her mother and grew up in foster care. She never knew her mother. Tiger is the name she used; it is a common tribal name, but a lot of folks believe Jack Jenson is her father.

"Why."

"Because he watched out for her and he was practically the only man in town who didn't sleep with her." Estelle gave me a look that assumed I was in the 'sleep with her' group.

"Any other reason?" I asked, sensing she was holding something back. Something substantial.

"She had his smile. That picture you have," she pointed to the photo. "It was taken by Jack at church. It was special to Nina."

"Look," I said, handing her another twenty. "I'd appreciate it if you didn't mention me to Officer Burton or Andy Valdez. Especially about the picture."

"Well, I ain't going to lie to the police, but if Tom doesn't ask, my lips are sealed."

"What about Andy?"

She looked out the hall window above the stairs to the street below and smiled. "That might be harder."

"Look, I'm out of twenties."

"Yea, well you are out of luck then, because Andy is standing outside with two of his buddies." She pointed out the hall window behind me.

"Is there a back way out?"

"Not unless you can fly."

"Well, I still expect you to say nothing about the picture."

"Sure, Honey. Say hi to Andy for me."

I wondered if she had called him. Walking down the stairs, I put the picture in my back pocket and kept my hands loose at my sides.

On the street, I stood in front of the coin wash, looking around as if getting my bearings or adjusting to the sun. Standing there, I made eye contact with Saul and George in the truck and then turned to look at Andy and his crew standing in front of a white convertible Mercedes. If Andy started anything, Saul would have the advantage of coming up on their flank.

Andy was nothing like I expected. He was very light skinned, more Spaniard. His hair was almost blond. He was small and compact, my height, five nine. He had on black jeans and a black Izod shirt. He was wearing high top black tennis shoes. His friends on the other hand, looked like Central American Indians, small, flat faced, pitch black hair, and pure muscle. Lightweights prize fighters dressed in black jeans, T-shirts, and wearing cowboy boots with silver toes. Perfect for kicking the shit out of someone in the wrong place. When they were half way across the street, I started walking towards them. Always take the attack to the enemy. Startled, they stopped at the curb as I continued across. By now, I had labeled the two bodyguards Heckle and Jeckle. Heckle was in the lead, long black hair in a ponytail and slightly taller. Jeckle was clearly the prizefighter type, crew cut hair, walking on his toes.

"Excused me, Mister," said Andy in an overdone Hispanic accent.

"Yes," I said, turning to face the two bodyguards.

"Where you been Bro?" asked Andy, as if we were long lost friends. Andy stood facing me. He had his feet set for a fight.

"Do I know you?" This caused Jeckle to move to the front, he was getting ready to deliver a sucker punch. Heckle reached inside his shirt.

Stopping to get my weight, distributed, I looked across the street and pointed, at a fence. Jeckle and Andy followed my gaze, allowing me time to kick Jeckle in the balls and move in close to Heckle. Grabbing his right hand inside his shirt, we struggled, until I heard Saul say, "Stop, or I'll put a bullet in your head."

Looking beyond Andy, Saul had a Colt .45 pressed against Heckle temple. George was standing by the truck with his hand inside the truck bed. Jeckle made to get up, but I kicked him again and shouted for him to stay down. At which point Andy told both men to stand down in Spanish.

"Look Mister, there must be some mistake," said Andy. "I asked you a simple question and you and your buddy attacked my friends. I don't think the Immokalee police are going to take very well to citizens being attacked by armed strangers." Now Andy sounded like Charleston Hesston pretending to be a Mexican cop in Touch of Evil.

"Drop the bullshit accent Andy. I know who you are, and my guess is you know who I'm," I said.

"Perhaps, but, what I don't know is why you are here and what you are doing nosing into something that doesn't concern you," said Andy.

"That might have been a fair question, had you and your buddies not been waiting in my house the other night armed to the teeth. See, I don't like uninvited visitors. And, I don't like seeing a friend bleed out, shot by a punk. So, I have a problem."

"Yea, what's your problem?"

"Whether I can afford to let you live. See, I already have enough to worry about. I don't need you."

"Funny, I've the same problem. Because of you, the police on my ass."

If he was afraid, he hid it well. He looked at me like I was already dead. "Perhaps we should talk with your Uncle. I heard that people around here often seek out his advice."

"And, they do what he tells them." Laughed Andy.

"He's a businessman. Perhaps he will see a way for us to declare a truce, because I for one do not need a war. A war you and your friends will not survive." At this, Saul cocked the .45, and Heckle said "por favor, no disparen."

Andy and I drove in the Mercedes, Saul and George followed in the Truck with Juan and Chico, in the back. Before getting into Andy's Mercedes, Saul handed me the Colt and George pulled an identical gun out from his belt. As usual, they had come prepared.

It took fifteen minutes to reach the farm. On the ride, I asked Andy to tell me about him and Nina. Andy liked hearing himself talk, he boasted about Nina, speaking openly about the drugs, sex, and their frequent fights. The more he talked, the more I realized he was well educated and rather cultured, and that he probably loved Nina. When I asked him about his Uncle, he smiled and said better that I should wait and see.

The main farm was over three hundred acres of scrub turned into lettuce and cornfields by irrigation. The main house was in the style of a Spanish villa with a circular drive leading up to a front courtyard. A hacienda that rivaled the mansions in Grosse Pointe where I grew up. Parking at the front door, Andy and I got out together. Juan and Chico jumped out and walked towards the back of the house. Saul and George waited by the truck.

Inside the house was cool, with marble floors and central air. In the front foyer, the marble floors continued up the stairs to the second floor. An older man wearing a white jacket greeted us in the foyer. I had the impression he was a servant. The two men spoke in Spanish, faster than I could understand. When they were finished, Andy said, "My Uncle is with his accountant. He will meet with us in a minute. We are to wait in the big library.

Andy was not exaggerating. We walked to a paneled double door. Opening the door for Andy, we stepped into a thirty by forty foot room filled from floor to ceiling with books. The diversity of titles and topics was impressive. Pulling out Hemmingway's *A movable feast*; I noted it was signed, 'to Frank'.

I'm not sure what I expected Frank to look like, perhaps a Latin Don Corleone. Instead, he was a small-distinguished looking man in his fifties, with gray hair and wearing suit pants, dress shirt, and a suit vest. His thinning head of hair was jet black with streaks of silver not gray. His clothes looked as if they were carefully selected; his pants had a razor crease. He was a man who took pride in his appearance. When he walked into the room, I noticed he was wearing what I took to be Ferragamo dress loafers. Shoes I knew cost three hundred plus.

Stepping in front of me, Andy spoke to his uncle in Spanish, saying something about nosing around and attacked. The only English he used was Colt .45. When Andy finished his uncle gestured for Andy to sit in a chair and then he approached me with an outstretched right hand. His small hand was warm and firm.

"Mister Cederberg. Please have a seat. May I offer you coffee or a glass of wine, a sherry perhaps?" When I indicated no, he sat in a hardback chair facing me.

"Andy tells me you have been asking questions about the unfortunate death of his finance, Nina Tigre. He says your man pulled a gun on him and his companions. That you attacked his friends and threatened his life. He thinks we should go to the police."

"He is welcome to call the police. I suggested it at Nina's, but we came here to see what you suggest, Mister Valdez?"

"I think men should solve their problems without the government. Also, I know there are two sides to every story, so I'm anxious to hear your side of this dispute." Valdez spoke like a lawyer arguing before a jury in a court case. "Please." He leaned forward in the chair.

"Two weeks ago I saw a girl swimming at midnight. I believed she was going to kill herself. I intervened. The girl was Nina. She told me she'd had a fight with her boyfriend because he asked her to perform oral sex on his friends. I walked her to her car and called the police, because I was concerned her boyfriend might be waiting for her at my beach house."

"Ah, you live on the beach, how nice."

"Yes, well, when the police arrived there was a gun fight and one of the officers was killed and another wounded. Whoever was in my house escaped."

"What happened to the girl?"

"I let her go."

"But then you came to Immokalee and went to see Jack Jenson."

"I must say, you are very well informed. The girl mentioned she worked at Jack's. I drove to Immokalee the next day to be sure she was all right.

"A girl you had never met before?" said Andy, ignoring his Uncle.

"I'm that kind of guy. Anyway, Jack told me she was gone, and I left."

"But here you are again." Frank Valdez, spread his hands out in a gesture as if he had just won a point of law.

"I had business with Jack. I stopped at Nina's apartment, for reasons I cannot exactly explain. I liked her and her death did not seem right." A sadness I cannot explain overwhelmed me. "I just wanted to be sure that the overdose was her doing, not caused by someone else. I don't like loose ends."

"You wondered if someone, perhaps Andy gave her the drugs that killed her?" said Valdez.

"I did. I learned one of Andy's boys was with Nina right before she died. It sounds like he left her on the floor."

"Would it surprise you to learn Andy came to me just three days ago and asked the same thing? You see, whatever you believe about my nephew, he loved this girl, and he too wondered if someone had sold her bad drugs or administered an overdose."

"What did you tell him?"

"The same thing I'm going to say to you. Nina Tigre was troubled. She was a drug addict and overdose by her own hand. No foul play, no conspiracy, no hit. Just a sad and tragic end to a young, beautiful girl's life. Taken for a reason only God knows." I watched him in this pronouncement, and I wondered if he had gone one-step too far. He was acting, but I was not sure if it was for Andy or me.

"Now we have to discuss you two. The last thing I want is a blood feud. In my experience, it is the innocents who are harmed the most, friends, and family. Your parents live in Naples, am I right?"

"Yes," I said starting to rise.

"So does Andy's mother. What a small world." He leaned closer and spoke in a whisper. "Mister Cederberg, you strike me as a man who finishes what he starts. As you said, no loose ends." He took a moment to glance at Andy.

"I understand that you and your friends in the truck have a gun club in Ft. Myers. I learned you have a police record and yet you are friends with the police."

"Mister Valdez," I said, "All I want is to go back to my business, but this girl Nina, her death, bothers me."

"Yes, and now Andy and you have crossed wires and both of you are still fully charged. I can see it, feel it." He looked at me and then Andy.

"Andy does not understand who you are, but I do. I checked on you, Mister Cederberg." The small man sat back and looked from me to Andy. For reasons I can't explain, he commanded respect.

"Please call me Robert," I offered.

"Robert, where you go, death follows. I hear you are a decent man. A peaceful man who is capable of violence. You were hoping the privacy of your house and beach would protect you. Now you are out in the world again because of a girl. You are like Don Quixote. Do you know this story?" He leaned in watching for my reaction.

"I do." I said.

"So you left your castle to save a simple tavern girl. Nina Tigre is your Dulcinea del Toboso, and when you learn she is dead, you seek revenge. However, look around; there are no dragons or windmills to slay. Her death is of her own doing. I think you should go home and forget about this girl. Give up your quest before it is too late."

"What about Andy?"

"Andy will do as I say. Provided you stay out of Immokalee."

"But, I've friends here, customers," I said. "I was even thinking about opening a gun store here is Immokalee."

"Whatever else we need here, more guns are not needed. We have plenty. If you want to visit Immokalee again, I suggest you call me first."

"You must know I could never agree to that condition, however, I've no plans to return here, and I'm happy to stay in Ft Myers and mind my own business provided your nephew and his crew agree to the same."

"Andy."

"Yes, Uncle."

"Do you hear what Mister Cederberg has agreed to?"

"Yes, he will stay out of Immokalee."

"And, what about you nephew?"

"I will stay out of Captiva."

"Good, now Andy I want you to go. I want to talk more with Mister Cederberg." Andy left the room without a word.

"He is a problem," said the Don.

"I can see that."

"He is not that tough, so I hired men to protect him."

"They make him think he is tough, his actions are based on their muscle, not his," I said.

"Yes, that is the problem. He's also wild and angry. He picks fights he cannot finish. This girl, Nina. She was all wrong for him. She was a drug addict, a prostitute. She made him wilder. He is better off without her, but he does not believe this. He blames you and he blames me."

"Why does he blame me?"

"Because you told her to run, and she was packing when he caught up with her. She was going to leave."

"Did he kill her?"

"No, as far as I know, her overdose was her own doing."

"But, you are worried her death will gnaw at him."

"When I die, Andy and my other nephews will take over a business that requires much finesse. You understand this word, finesse."

"I think so."

"I've no children, only a dead brother and sister and my three nephews. I loved my brother, but he was wild, he drank. Now all that is left of him are his two sons. Stephan, Andy's brother is the oldest. He is twenty-four and shows promise. He has a head for business and is taking classes at the college in Naples. Andy is like his father, wild, what you call a hothead. He does not understand negotiation and compromise. Andy has never worked a real job on his own. He runs errands for me. He wants to be a gangster and pimp. He wants to carry machine guns and drive foreign cars, like in the movies."

"What about your other nephew?" I asked.

Don Valdez got up and walked to a couch opposite me. "At my core," he said, "I'm a farmer. I come to this barren scrubland, this land with water underneath. I nurture the land and grow food for my family. A farmer understands hard work and sacrifice. Today,

63

I'm many things, but at my core, I'm a farmer, Mister Cederberg, and now I wonder, what are you?"

He asked this last question softly. So quietly, a jury would have to lean in to hear. So sincere, there could be no doubt he wanted to know. He made me feel as if my answer was important to him, yet I had no immediate answer. I don't know what I'm at my core, unless it is 'a shooter.'

"I've never been sure, Don Valdez. When I was a boy, I was called the Turtle, because I was cautious. I stayed in my shell and kept my head down, and watched. Now, like you, I'm a businessman and I am good at my business. I know guns. I sell guns. I'm a champion target shooter. I've been a shooter since I was a boy. At my core, I guess I am still the Turtle."

"But, every once in a while, you come out of your shell. Something or someone draws you out into the real world. Like this girl Nina."

"Yes"

"So, what does the Turtle become when he leaves his shell?"

"I don't know, really? I only know that people die."

"Yes, that is closer to the truth. You bring death. I don't mean you are literally death; you don't wear a black robe and carry a scythe. However, when you leave your shell, people die. I think you are a bringer of death, a killer."

"Don Valdez, there is nothing unusual about me, nothing exceptional or unique. I learned how to shoot guns at an early age and I do that well. I served in the army, and learned how to kill and

I do that well. However, I've no need for violence or death. I'm not a psychopath. I don't have my mother in the basement. I live on the beach because it brings me peace. I live a quiet life that includes work and friends. I've been forced to kill, to protect myself, but I'm not a killer." Even as I said this, I wondered at its truth. I was denying the obvious, the facts. There were dozens of graves in Vietnam because of me, several in Michigan, and more in Florida. Looking at the older man, I suddenly understood why I was there.

"Don Valdez, you think I'm a hired killer, a pro. I'm not. You wonder if I've been hired to kill you and your family. Again, no. I'm not an assassin. I'm not a professional. I'm not a hit man."

"Robert, it is you who misunderstands. I know you aren't a professional. However, I wonder if you want to be? So often in my business, I've the need of a man with military experience, a professional. A man who can evaluate a situation and tell me what is needed. A man who can think on his own, but one who will follow instructions, carry out a mission, and not ask questions or feel anything when he is done. I was wondering if you and your friends outside are such men. Because if you are, there is considerable money that can be made. I've friends who need guns, machine guns, and other weapons used by armies. I need men with military experience fighting in jungles."

"There are plenty of men who sell such guns already."

"In South America or Africa, but not right here. I need someone I can trust. Someone who can teach us to use the new guns."

"And once in a while someone who can use a gun!" I added.

"Yes, exactly. A man under contract."

"For drug money. Illegal money. Money from crime."

"Money is money."

"I think I'd prefer being Don Quixote."

"Are you sure?"

"I run a gun club. All I want to do is teach people to shoot. Send your men to me with a legal gun and I will teach them. Nothing more."

"Are you sure?"

"Yes."

"Let's leave it at that. If I send my men to you for instruction, you will teach them?"

"Saul and George will be happy to teach your men."

"And what about automatic weapons. Machine Guns?"

"Not at the Club. However, private lessons on private land are fine by me."

"So you will teach my men?"

"No, I think I will have to pass, but Saul or George can do what they like. I'm going back to my beach and stay there."

"Wise choice I'm sure, but not what I hoped. After all, you taught Jack Jenson and his boys."

"Talk to Saul," I said, leaving it there.

I was convinced Frank Valdez would keep his word and I wanted to believe Nina's death was an accident. Driving home, I told

Saul, and George about Valdez' offer. George said no immediately. Saul said he have to think about it.

~*~

Saul Bernstein fought in the Tet Offensive. He was a transplanted New York Jew, with no real religion other than the cult Cocaine and the Colt .45. He loved drugs and guns and was a genius when it came to repairing a sticking slide or misaligned sight. He was a field appointed sergeant destined to be broken down to private had he stayed in the Army.

When Saul arrived back in the world, he spent three weeks in Brooklyn before his family and his old life forced him to decide. Before being drafted, Saul was selling televisions during the day in his uncle's electronics and camera shop on Flatbush Avenue. At night and on the Sabbath he sold marijuana.

Before going to Vietnam, Saul was a happy go lucky guy who sold just enough dope to keep himself in weed. When he returned to Brooklyn, someone else controlled the marijuana trade and cocaine was just taking off. When Saul came home, he was a man familiar with illegal drug sales and only felt whole when he was carrying a gun. After several failed attempts to get a straight job, he offered his talents to the local corner boss, a man who saw in Saul a man he could depend on.

Saul stands six feet tall; he is thin, but fit, with dark features, and a classic Jewish face, with deep-set eyes, too large a nose, and big ears. At home in Brooklyn, he wore a Yakama taped to his head, because of his Army buzz cut. On the street, he looked like a Jewish

Hell's Angel wearing black jeans, black turtleneck, and a black leather vest.

According to Saul, Roscoe Geonellia took one look at Saul and hired him as a personal bodyguard. Roscoe was the local mafia member who controlled the drugs and dealers in Saul's neighborhood. He ran a network of street vendors. Saul's job was to prevent the vendors from stepping out of line. Roscoe made his office at the Veterans & Friends Social Club on 86th St. in Bensonhurst. Two different hoods frisked Saul and a third questioned him before he met with Geonellia.

"What you want," Roscoe asked.

"I want a job Mister Geonellia."

"Go talk to Hyme Silverstein."

"I spoke with Mister Silverstein, but I felt working for him might endanger my health."

"Why is that?"

"Because no one frisked me before I met with Mister Silverstein. He is too trusting. Too careless. I'm a careful man. I want to work for someone with a future." This last statement made Roscoe laugh, because he already knew he was going to hit Silverstein.

"You are a Jew, asking to work for an Italian. What happens if things get rough, can I depend on you?

"The only loyalty I have is to my family and friends and money."

"Nothing else? What about America? I heard you were in Vietnam."

"Before I went to Vietnam, I loved my country. I was proud to fight for America. Now, I'm not so committed. All I want right now is a job and some money in my pocket."

"So go work for your uncle. Sell TVs. You know what they say, don't do the crime unless you are prepared to serve the time. You are a war hero. Get a straight job, find a girl."

"That is good advice, except I ain't no hero. The Army taught me to fight and kill and Vietnam taught me how to sell drugs. This is all I know."

"Okay, I'll give you a try. I need a man with muscle and brains. You seem to have both. Be here on Monday at ten in the morning and I will give you a try."

After three months, Saul was collecting weekly payments from street vendors and guarding Roscoe during drug buys. Earning a thousand a week, Saul was able to purchase all the cocaine his habit required. However, when a drug deal went bad on Roscoe, Saul ran until he bumped into me at the Green Parrot. A year later, as we drove back to Ft. Myers, I knew the job at the gun club was good for Saul, but I also knew he missed the kind of action Don Valdez was offering.

After talking it over, Saul contacted Frank Valdez and agreed to instruct his men in the use of any guns Frank purchased from the Bullseye. I gave my blessings to the deal because we were not supplying any automatic weapons. It seemed ironic that Saul should be training both sides in a future land war, but he was confident that it was the smart move. When I talked to him about working for Frank Valdez, he said the Don Valdez was a lot like Roscoe Geonellia, very old school; a man who believed in family, honor, and loyalty. When I asked about Andy, Saul said the kid was just another junkie punk, adding in his opinion the real problem was Boca. If Saul thought Boca was dangerous, I needed to pay attention.

BLOOD TRAILS
Chapter 5

For me, Immokalee became a name in the news and Nina became another loose end. In the weeks that followed, I return to my routine, running the club, teaching gun safely, watching and waiting. In short, I climbed back into my shell.

On Sundays, I like to take the morning off to walk the beach. In June, the beach doesn't become too hot or too crowded before eleven in the morning. I was just coming into the house when the phone rang.

"Mister Cederberg?"

"Yes, that's right."

"Mister Cederberg, this is Sergeant Martin Hill with the Naples Police."

"What can I do for you, Sergeant?"

"Do you still have family in Naples?"

"Yes, my Mother and Father live in East Naples."

"Eric and Caroline Cederberg."

"Yes, has something happened?"

"Mister Cederberg, when was the last time you talked to your parents?"

"I saw them at Christmas."

"Six months ago."

"Yes, we aren't very close."

"Have you talked to them recently?"

"No."

"I'm sorry to have to tell you, but your mother and father are in Naples Community Hospital."

"What happened?"

"A neighbor called the police saying their house didn't look right. When a patrol car checked, they found the house open. The officers on the scene found considerable blood in one of the bathrooms, but your parents were gone. Naturally we checked the hospitals, but it took time to fine them?"

"Are they all right?"

"I spoke with your mother this morning. She will be fine, but her story was very confused."

"What about my dad?"

"He is in intensive care. It seems they had a car accident that went unreported. We are still trying to understand what happened at their house. I was hoping you might know. Can I ask where you were last night?"

"I haven't been in Naples if that is what you are asking. I was at work all Friday and yesterday I was out on the water with a woman I met. She is staying at South Seas Plantation. I can give you her number if you like. Could my parents been attacked?" I asked, thinking about the Don's promise.

"Do you know of anyone who might want to harm your parents?"

"I had some trouble a while back, but they aren't a part of it, my mother is a house wife, and my dad works part time at the Scotty's by their house. They are retired."

"Might they have cash or valuable hidden in the house?"

"Obviously, you haven't seen where they live."

"Actually, I've been in the house, and I understand what you mean, but the patrol report said it looks like a hit went down."

"Should I go there?"

"No, you should go see to your mother and father. After that we can meet at the house if you want."

"What about my brothers? Have they been contacted?"

"How many brothers do you have?

"Three."

"Is there any reason to believe any of your brothers are in Naples?"

"No, but we haven't talked in quite some time."

"Will you call your brothers, just to be sure?"

"Do you think my parents were attacked?"

"Given your history, it is the first thing we considered."

"My parents have nothing to do with any of that."

"These recent troubles. As I understand it, an officer was shot by intruders in your house, and Frank Valdez was mentioned."

"I told the Captiva police everything I knew. I'm certain that there is no one after me, and no one who would harm my parents."

"How can you be so certain?"

"Because I spoke to Frank Valdez and he assured me the event was an accident and nothing more like it would happen."

"Well, I know you will want to see your parents and talk to your brothers. Perhaps when you know more, you will call me."

I spent the next hour on the phone talking to my brothers Austin and John. My brother Bill did not answer his phone, which only made me more worried. When I got hold of Austin, he said he was going to talk to the police and he kept asking me, what I had done. I could tell he assumed someone attacked our parents because of me. Frankly, I suspected the same thing, but it pissed me off that he jumped to that conclusion immediately.

I caught John on his way to play golf. When I explained why I was calling, he said wanted to fly down and be with me. An offer I appreciated, but I was uncertain how he could help. If my family was in danger, I did not want him in Florida. In the end, I convinced him to wait a day until I knew more. When I asked John about Bill. He said lately Bill had been adrift. He had been through several jobs and girlfriends, each ending because of him.

At the Club, I saw George's Honda 350 was in the lot, as was Saul's pickup. Entering through the back, I found George cleaning the glass counter top on the pistol case and Saul sweeping the lobby floor. Both men were wearing their shooting vests, a sign they were armed.

"What did you find out," asked George.

"My brother Bill is not answering his phone."

"What about your parents?"

"They are in Naples Community. I'm going there first, after I will want to see the house."

"I'm going with you," said Saul.

"We both are," said George.

"I wish I knew about Bill."

"How about his friends?" suggested Saul. "Do you know any of his buddies, friends from work? Someone you can call."

"I hate to admit this," I said, "but I know nothing about his life. My brother John has gone over to his house to check. I'm not even sure where he lives. I talk with my brothers two or three times a year on the phone and mainly we talked about Eric and Caroline. John and Austin have kids, I've never met."

"Robert, this isn't the time," said George. "Becoming a real brother or a good son will have to wait,

"It is too late for that," I sighed.

"It doesn't matter. Right now, your brothers need a point man. Someone who will take charge and get answers. What do we do when our intelligence is faulty?"

"Send out a recon team."

"Right now, you need a recon. We need to talk to your mom and then we need to check out your parent's house."

"I will pack for a trip to Naples," said Saul.

Detective Hill was on another line when I called. When he came on the phone, he agreed to meet me at the hospital at one. I did not bother to mention I was bringing George and Saul.

We drove to Naples in my truck. Before we left, Saul spent some time on the phone and then he put a shotgun in the truck tool chest. My parents live on the east side of Naples. From Ft. Myers there is really only one way, down through Bonita and Vanderbilt beach to Naples. Along the way, we talked about the building that was taking place west of highway forty-one. High rises on the beach and new communities set back behind the canals, five or six blocks from the beach, places like Naples Park.

There are two hospitals in Naples, but Naples Community Hospital in downtown Naples was the hospital most people used. I had been to the hospital once to visit Tim Wilson before he died. Detective Hill was waiting in a patrol car when we arrived. I had not seen Martin Hill in a year or more, but he looked the same, fit and compact, with a barrel chest; he was the picture of a no nonsense cop.

Generally, I hate hospitals; there are just some things I can't face. At the reception desk, I learned my parents were on different floors. Eric was in a critical care recovery room on the third floor. Caroline was on the second floor in the general wing. We went to see her first.

Caroline was sitting up in bed watching television. She was wearing a hospital gown. "Robert, where have you been? How do I look?" "Have you seen your father? What about Bill?"

"Bill! Is Bill here?"

"Of course he is. Don't be silly."

"Mom, what happened?"

"We had an accident."

"What kind of accident?"

"A car crash."

"You were in a car accident?"

"We hit a tree."

"Did you tell that to the police?"

"Of course not!"

"What happened in the house? A Detective called and said there is blood all over the bathrooms." At this point, my mom started to cry.

"Oh Robert…"

"Tell me what happened." Behind me, Sergeant Hill took a seat, but Saul and George left the room.

"Bill came for a visit. He lost another job. Your father and he had a terrible fight. Your father was drinking. Bill left and drove off. We heard him when he came home, but we kept our bedroom door closed. I made Eric lock the door. We heard Bill in the kitchen watching TV. Then he tried our door and when it would not open, he started pounding the door, screaming and crying. He even called me mommy."

"What happened then?" asked Hill.

"Billy went crazy. He kept pounding on the door. After the second or third time I made Eric go out through the porch door and back in the kitchen so he could talk to Bill. The next thing I know, the door came off the hinges and Bill and your father are rolling around on the floor and then Bill and your father are bleeding. I tried to stop the bleeding, but I could not get it to stop so we drove to the hospital, and on the way we hit a car and then drove into that tree." She took a moment to gather herself.

"Mom, how did Dad and Bill get cut?"

"I don't want to talk about it. What about your father? Did they say when we can go home?"

"I don't know yet. Why didn't you call me? Why didn't Bill call?"

"He didn't want you to know. Your brother has a lot of pride. He came down here to get free of drugs."

"Right, I said "and the first thing he does is put you and dad in the hospital.

"You know I blame that girl of his, that Lisa. She drank a lot."

"What are you talking about? Bill's problem isn't drinking! Its marijuana and cocaine. He was selling dope in high school, before he met Lisa."

"Don't be ridiculous. He was a good boy before Lisa."

"Mom, you are talking crazy. Lisa was ten years ago," I said, being less than diplomatic. I never want to argue with my mother, but then she will say some outrageous statement and I will correct her, and the battle begins.

"Robert, what happened to you?" she asked. She started to cry. I gave her a timid hug, but then she pushed away. "You use to be such a nice boy."

I thought for a moment, some of what she said was true, I was different and so was Bill. I live a different life from my family and with me it is out of sight out of mine. I seldom thought about my brothers or parents because they were out of sight. On the few occasions the whole family was together, we lived in the past.

"Robert, have you seen your father?"

"No, I came to see you first."

"He didn't feel good when we arrived. He hit his head in the crash. We all did, packed in that little car. I'm worried about your father. Will you check on him?" She started crying again.

"Of course." I said, kissing her on the head. Sergeant Hill and I left the room.

"What do you think?" I asked.

"You go find your father. I'm going to talk to your mom again, but it sounds like a simple domestic fight. I will wait here for you. Take your time. When you have finished we can go out to the house if needed. He put his arm around my shoulder. "It will be alright," he said.

My dad was on a different floor in a critical care room. George was sitting in the waiting room. "Robert, they won't let me see him. Only family. I started to tell them I was Austin, but I didn't want to cause you trouble. I asked how he is, and they would not say. That isn't good."

"It is okay George. Go sit with my mother. She is starving for company."

My dad was asleep, unconscious, with a dozen tubes and monitors on his head and chest. His thin gray hair was unkempt with a white stubble was on his chin. The nurse said they were worried about brain and spinal injury. They were keeping Dad in a drug-induced coma so he would sleep and not move. They said he was up and walking earlier and then he fell down and said he could not move his feet.

Taking a chair, I combed his thinning hair and squeezed his hand. Leaning, I whispered that I was there with him and he would be fine. Throughout my stay, he mumbled and talked in his sleep and his eyes rolled and raced back and forth. For a second, he awoke and asked me, "If we were rich?"

I stayed about ten minutes, squeezing his hand, but there was nothing I could do. A doctor at the nurses' station explained that he was worried that Dad had blood on the brain and might have a spinal injury. The doctor said the next three days would determine whether he lived and regained his brain and spinal functions. In describing my dad's condition, he asked if I had any experience with disabled adults and brain injury. When I shook my head no, he suggested I visit the patient information desk in the main lobby.

It took me a while to find Bill. The door to the wing where his room was located was locked. On the door, it said 'Psychiatric Unit.' Saul was sitting in a blue chair by the door talking to an older nurse. When he saw me jumped up.

"He's in detox," he said as the nurse left.

"Do you know her?"

"No, but she is sweet. Very helpful. How is your dad?"

"Bad, he might wind up in a wheel chair. What about Bill?"

"Standard thirty day Psych evaluation. It is lucky the police were not involved. He cut his hands and arms fighting with your dad. When your mom came in, she said she was in a car accident. I guess she didn't mention your father and brother were unconscious in the car. The nurse said Bill is lucky he did not bleed out. These people up here know what is what, but Bill is under lock and key, so they have time. He is still unconscious."

"What does that mean?"

"Robert, listen to me. Your brother nearly bled out. His brain may have been injured. However, the nurse I was talking to said he has a good chance. If I were you, I'd call John and Austin. They must be going nuts."

"What will I do if Bill or Dad is handicapped?"

"All I know is what it is like for guys in the VA."

"I rather someone kills me than wind up in a wheelchair"

"You say that, but plenty of vets live through it."

"All I'm saying is,"

"Don't say it," said a voice behind us. It was George. "Hospitals are bad places. They bring out the worst; never say anything you might regret. Wait until you are away from here."

"I've got to go and look at their house. What happened to Sergeant Hill?"

"He's gone. He told me after talking to your mom the house was no longer an official crime scene. Your mom had a set of keys in her purse. We can go see the house whenever we want."

"No time like the present," said Saul.

~*~

Turning into Flamingo Estates, I was struck by how much the neighborhood had changed in only five years. Once, all the houses on Robin Lane were well kept, newly painted ranch homes, with nice lawns and few with pools. Now, there were several houses on the block that looked like they had been taken over by squatters, the paint was faded, roofs damaged, five cars in the driveway.

My parent's house was the second off the corner. At one time, the house had a garage, but the first owner turned the garage into a family room, replacing the garage door for a sliding door. The side door into the family room had yellow police tape across it. Inside, there were two couches and two easy chairs all facing a television. At the back of the room were the washer and dryer. This was the room where my parents spent most of their time.

Entering the house I was hit with the smell of dogs and blood, neither stronger than the other. The family room looked as it always did; it was messy and lived in. My dad had a habit of taking things from somewhere else, a shelf, a cupboard, the bedroom and bringing the thing into the   family room to read or look at and then he would leave it on a couch, a table or the floor and there it would stay like it had always been there. An open briefcase and a camera were in the same spot on the couch where dad set them two years ago Christmas.

The house had green shag carpet, which might have been popular and attractive when my dad bought the house, but now it looked like something you needed boots to walk on. Moving into the kitchen, I saw that nothing was changed or seemed amiss. The kitchen and dining room and living room all looked the same, same carpet, same clutter. There was the usual pile of bills in a chafing dish, and the pipes my dad no longer smoked on the television. Moving into the front room, where the good furniture sat untouched, I saw the first traces of blood on the carpet and stopped.

"They went out the front door," said Saul pointing to the trail of blood pooled at the front door. Walking in single file, we moved to the back of the house, to the guest bathroom and the two bedrooms.

The master bedroom door was broken off its hinges. There was more blood in the master bathroom. In the hallway between the two bedrooms, there was a trail of blood leading out of my parents' bedroom to the guest bathroom. The bathroom door was open with yellow tape across the door. Blood was spattered all over the shag carpet and on the mirror over the sinks. Across from my parent's bedroom was the guest room or what we called the "boys" room.

The guest bedroom door had a decal of an airplane that said "boys" on the wooden door. It had been there when my parents moved in and since they considered the guest bedroom the "boys" room they left the decal up. The fact that we were all adult men, and that we never slept in the same room did not change the image for them. In the boys' room there were two twin beds, the bed against the far wall was unmade. There was a suitcase in the closet. In addition, there were clothes hanging in the closet. On the nightstand between the two single beds there were several books, war histories and autobiographies.

"It does look like a crime scene," said George.

"Bill broke in the door. They fought in the hall and then tried to stop the bleeding in both bathrooms."

"There is less blood than I expected," said Saul. "I'm surprised the police thought this was a hit"

"Still, it's going to take a lot to clean this place," said George.

"I would do the whole thing. Pull the carpet, paint, everything while they are out of the house," added Saul.

"Do you know anyone?" I asked.

"Let's go see B.J.," said Saul.

~*~

The River Walk Ale house is inside Tin City on Naples Bay. In amongst T-shirt and shell shops, women's clothing and jewelry stores, the River Walk is a haven for tourists and locals. Inside, a large wooden horse shoe bar is surrounded by a single row of tables inside, and a row of tables on a boat deck outside. The décor is classic, Florida tourist: coiled ropes, skippers' wheel, oars, and a chalkboard with daily specials. Comparatively speaking, the fish and chips are good, the cold slaw creamy, and the bartender, Billy Jean or BJ was a Florida classic. That Sunday having spent the last hours in the hospital and then an eternity in my patent's house, BJ was a vision in khaki and Coppertone.

"Saulie," said Billie Jean, as we entered. She had on khaki shorts and a white shirt that said River Walk on it.

"Howdy Jean, he said.

"And George," she added, giving George as big smile. "Don't tell me," she stopped to look at me. "Can this be the famous Robert," she said, putting a cocktail napkin down in front of me. She had a pretty face, etched by too many late nights and too many days in the sun. She was very tan, which added to her beauty, but eventually her skin would be leather.

"Jean," said Saul, "Robert's parents are in the hospital. We need a drink."

"I'm so sorry Robert. Saulie talks about you all the time. I've been looking forward to meeting you. What can I get you?"

"I just want a beer, anything except a Bud. Will you have something?"

"Thanks, but it is still ice tea time for me. Maybe later. What happened to your parents?" she asked.

Telling the story, made me feel better. She was a good listener and a good bartender. When I described Bill, she said there was a young guy like that in the River Walk a week ago with an older couple.

"I knew he had a problem," she added.

"We all did," I said, "it's just that we did nothing about it."

"Some of us live out our lives trying to stay out of other people's lives," said George. "When I was injured, people said, you will get better. However, they were wrong. I did not get better, at least at first. People said, it will be all right, but it wasn't. I don't know what would have happened to me if Robert had not made it his business to help me."

"Unfortunately, I did nothing for my own brother," I said.

"It is never too late to start help people," offered BJ. She gave me a smile I hoped she reserved for only a few.

"While they are alive, it is never too late to help."

"I had a sister who died of cancer. She died before I even knew it was too late. So now, when I hear someone is sick or needs help, I try to do something, even if it is just bringing over a meal."

"BJ," I said, "I can see why Saul likes you so much. I hope someday I can be half the person you are." I got up to leave, laying a twenty on the table.

"Robert, whatever happens, don't lose this chance to make a difference with your family."

"What should I do?" I asked her.

"What does your mother need the most?"

"Someone to take care of her, I guess."

"And who will do that?"

"My brother John is on the way, as we speak. He will be here tomorrow or the day after. He is planning to take care of my mom."

"Why not you? Why don't you take care of her?"

"We don't get along. She does not approve of the Club and my guns. Neither of my parents do. When I moved down here my mom could not even wait for the dishes to dry before she started asking me when I was leaving. She wanted me out, and I wanted to get out."

"But, now things are different, she needs you. Why not stay at her house for a while?"

"You haven't seen it. It is a pit. If I stayed there I would have to clean the house and replace the carpet."

"So why not do that? Can you afford it?"

"Sure, but I can't do something like that without asking."

"Why not? Look, I've a friend who sells carpet. He could do the whole house in a day, and I'm sure he can arrange for a house cleaning. Afterwards, hire a painter to put on a fresh coat of paint and your parents have a new home."

"That sounds great; can you give me the number of your friend?"

"Of course, and make sure you mention me."

I called BJ's friend and arranged to look at carpet that afternoon. Once we had agreed on a carpet and color, he called a house cleaner and I arranged to meet a crew in the morning at the house. When I was done, Saul and George dropped me off at the house and then drove my truck home to Ft. Myers. If I needed a car, I could drive my parents 1978 Mercury Cougar.

Fortunately, the cleaners showed up before I had to spend too much time alone in the house. After considerable translations and a brief argument, I joined the crew in cleaning the house. Learning that the carpet was going to be replaced, they focused on the walls, the tile floors, the kitchen, furniture, and last but not least, the bathrooms.

I would have wagered that it was impossible to clean my parent's house ever, let alone in a few hours, but the five of us made a serious dent in washing and dusting. We even did two loads of laundry, the sheets and a hamper of dirty clothes. When we finished, I drove the Cougar to the hospital and spent time with my mother watching TV.

I told her about replacing the carpet and cleaning the house. I could not tell whether she was angry or pleased. Later, after Mom fell asleep, I spend an hour with my father, holding his hand. Before going home, I stopped in at the River Walk to see if BJ was still working. Learning she had gone home, I drove to a Publics grocery store to see about stocking up the house before John arrived.

BROTHERS
Chapter 6

My brother John called from Georgia to tell me he would be in Naples on Tuesday. We talked for only a minute or two about our parents' conditions and what I was doing to the house. When John asked what he could do, I suggested he stop at Penny or Sears and buy some new sheets and bed covers. Laughing, he asked where I would sleep until then. Getting off the phone, I thought about how ironic it was that my father worked at a hardware store and yet nothing in the house was fixed. On the patio table, there was a coil of caulking and a tool for installing screens. Working at the hardware, he knew what was needed to repair the lanai, but he never got around to repairing or replacing any screens.

The carpet men arrived at seven forty five in the morning and started moving furniture. The shag in the family room came up easily once the couches were on to the porch. I was amazed at the men's strength, and the fact that they did not wear gloves. Like the cleaning crew, the carpet men were all Hispanic, except the foreman, who was a pure Florida Cracker. For the new carpet, I selected light tan Berber wool with stain resistance. The carpet came in a huge roll that they cut outside. Admiring the speed and efficiency with which they worked I wondered if all these men would have arthritic knees when they were sixty.

I was enjoying a second cup of café Vienna when Saul showed up driving my truck. He said he was worried I needed the truck, but in fact, I realized he wanted to be there. Pouring himself a cup of instant coffee, he admitted he was planning to see the nurse from yesterday. Whatever his reason for being in Naples, we both knew George could run the Club without of us.

Moving our coffees outside to the porch, I mentioned that I wanted to visit my parents and see about Bill, but I was a little nervous about leaving the house full of workers. My parents are knick knack people. They have knickknacks from the various places my father visited. My mother always claimed they are valuable, to me they seem like junk. However, I knew we had a collection of Royal Dalton figures my grandmother owned. I did not really think the men would steal anything while I was gone; the problem was I would not know. When I voiced this, Saul said his usual, "Don't worry about it. I will work on the lanai while you visited your family."

Driving the Cougar to the hospital, I felt better about my life and the world than I ever had. I was not worried about the club, I was talking to my brothers, and I was doing something positive to help my parents while they were in the hospital.

Visiting hours began at eleven o'clock. When I walked into my mom's room her first question was "Where have you been?" She was up and dressed and waiting to go home. When I asked her if the doctors said she could go, she informed me, "It doesn't matter. The food is awful and I am leaving."

Saying I was going to find a doctor, I left my mother, fully dressed, and sitting on the bed. A nurse informed me that my mother was scheduled to be discharged at noon. When I asked her who she was discharging my mother to, she was at a loss. My father was a different story. He had taken a turn for the worse. According to his doctor, they had tried again to get my father to walk, but he could not control is legs. The doctor said he feared a thoracic injury, meaning that my dad might be able to use his arms and hands but nothing below his chest. If he lived, he would be a paraplegic.

As the doctor talked, I thought about the movies where war heroes come back in a wheelchair. Then I tried to see Eric in a wheelchair and Caroline taking care of him. Sitting with my dad, I struggled with how little we shared, how much there was about him that I did not know, and might never know.

At the Psychiatric Unit, I was told Bill was conscious and I could visit him, but only for ten minutes. The nurse said he was being restrained for his own good. When I asked her what we should talk about, she gave me a funny look. Trying again, I told her I was uncertain how to behave. "Like a brother," was her only advice.

Bill was pale and had lost considerable weight since I'd last seen him. His hair was long and his curly red beard needed a trim. He was asleep sitting up in bed, but his hands were in leather straps. Sitting down beside him, I realized it was over a year since we had talked, and here he was in Florida without me knowing. I watched him sleep for several minutes and then made to leave, when he asked, "Are you going to say something?"

"I didn't realize you were awake," I said.

"I come in and out."

"How are you?"

"Fucked," he laughed. "How are Mom and Dad?"

"Mom is dressed and ready to go home. She says she hates the food. So, what happened?"

"I don't remember much. It was really fucked up. Dad and I fought. I cannot remember what it was about. For some reason, Dad has a kitchen knife, and he cut me pretty badly. Mom wrapped us up in bath towels and we drove to the hospital. How is dad?"

"Not very good. Wait, what do you mean Dad had a knife?"

"I was pounding on their bedroom room and Dad came up behind me carrying a kitchen knife. He acted as if I was an intruder. He was afraid of me. He held the knife out as a threat."

"What did you do?"

"I tried to take the knife from him and we end up both being cut. How bad is Dad? Was he cut badly?"

"You had an accident on your way here. You hit a tree; nothing big, but Dad was injured and they did not realize it. Now they think it might be a spinal injury."

"You mean he is a cripple?" Bill started crying.

"He could be in a wheelchair, but it is early. We have to wait and see." Bill began crying and seemed like he might lose it, so I pressed his buzzer for a nurse. She was a young Hispanic woman with very short black hair. She made me think of Nina. Bill cried and struggled against his restraints. She spoke softly to him touching his head. Eventually he fell asleep.

"I told him about our father. The news is not good. I think he needs something," I whispered.

"I'm sorry," she said not seeming very sorry at all. "There is nothing prescribed for your brother." We are trying to eliminate all the drugs from his system, even ones we use here. The next three days will be very hard for him. He will need your support."

"I'll try," I said making my way for the door.

Back with my mother, the nurse informed both of us that my mother was all checked out and a wheelchair had been ordered to take her to the lobby. Out in front, I helped her into the Cougar, and then did not know where to take her. I knew the house with all the workman would upset her, so I considered a local motel. The problem with a motel, even though it made sense, was the fact that I owned a perfectly good house less than an hour away. Even as indifferent as I am to criticism and public opinion, I did not think I could explain to George or Saul, how it was I put my mother in a motel. When I discussed my plan with my mom, she solved the problem for me.

"I can't live on Captiva," she said. "I have to visit your father and brother every day. I need to go to the house."

"But it is being painted," I offered lamely.

"Fine, take me to a motel; I will stay at a motel tonight."

Seizing the opportunity, I took her to a Comfort Inn near the house. I returned to her house to get her clothes and her toiletries, while she stayed in the motel watching television.

Saul was drinking beer and eating chips with the carpet crew supervisor when I arrived. The workmen were sitting in a truck out in front. Inside, the carpet was down, and the screens were finished.

"I just need your signature that we completed the work as agreed and a check," he said.

"Well, it looks great," I added. "I see you even changed the layout of the furniture."

"That was Saul's doing. He said the house needed a complete change."

"What about the painters? Are you in charge of them too?"

"Sorry, I don't know anything about painters. You should call the office."

Learning they had not arranged for painters, Saul told me he would take care of everything and I should go and be with my family. The trouble was I did not want to see my mother again, let alone Dad or Bill. When I admitted how I felt to Saul, he took me to pick up Caroline and the three of us went to Sears to buy paint. Afterwards Saul and I took Caroline to Giuseppe's for pizza and then after dropping her at the motel, we went back to the house to paint.

We were painting the last room, the family room when John arrived. It was ten in the morning on Tuesday. "John, thank God you are here," I declared, hugging my younger brother. John was the tallest of the brothers, nearly five ten. He was a runner and had a lean, fit body. I thought of John as a rock. He was dependable. With him in Naples, I assumed I could go back to the Club and he would take care of Mom and Dad.

"Robert, what's with you hugging?" he said pushing me away.

"I'm just glad to have another brother here."

"Well, don't get too used to it because I've to go back on Saturday."

"But, this is Tuesday."

"I know, but I could only get off a week of work, and it took me two days to get here. Better, hand me a cup of coffee and a paint brush, because we are wasting time."

We talked as we painted. Saul made the beds using the new sheets and bedspreads that John purchased at Penny and then promptly went to sleep on one of the single beds in the boys' room.

Naturally, John was anxious to see Mom and Dad, but he seemed most concerned about Bill. They were only two years apart and grew up as playmates and friends, sharing much more than I did with Austin. We debated taking Mom with us. I said we should leave her, but John insisted that we take mom. In the long run, it worked out because she sat with Dad when John and I went to see Bill.

This time Bill was sitting up and out of his restraints. He had better color, and he as eating red Jell-O. Seeing John, Bill started to cry, and I worried we'd need another nurse.

"John, I'm so glad you are here." Bill smiled and reached out to John for a hug. Leaning in I hugged my two brothers, but I already felt left out. They shared something I would never have.

"How are you doing," I asked.

"My doctor is really good and the nurses are great. I'm hoping I can really turn my life around. Tomorrow I start my group therapy session. The Doc is cool. He really understands how hard it can be. He is an ex-user."

"What about you," I asked Bill.

"What do you mean, Robert?" asked John.

"I mean, where is Bill in all this?"

"Robert, this can wait," said John giving me a look.

"I'm sorry, but we never talk about Bill's problems. Dad is in the hospital because of Bill, and I want to know if he accepts his responsibility.

"Of course I do. I got high and made a mistake."

"Mistake," I shouted. "What the fuck are you talking about? You went crazy. You fought with Dad.   You hit a tree and now Dad will never walk again." I knew I was being stupid. I knew I should shut up. I was burning bridges right when I needed to build bridges. Bill started crying.

"Robert, I wasn't driving that night."

"What?" I said, having to sit down

"Mom was driving. Dad and I couldn't drive, so Mom drove. Right before the hospital, she hit a car or a truck and then served into that tree in front. She should never have tried to drive because of her sight."

"What's wrong with her sight?" asked John, before I could.

"She is going blind. Didn't she tell you? There is something wrong with her retina. Last month she hit a mailbox." After this announcement, we settled down and talked like brothers.

After a time, John said he wanted to spend time alone with Bill and I left to find mom. Before leaving, I apologized to Bill saying I was sorry, but the truth was still blamed Bill for what had happened.

Walking down to the critical care floor, I thought about all the questions I had, why they did not call 911 from the house, and why my mom didn't tell me she was driving or about her sight. Then it hit me, my mom was going blind and my dad was handicapped, and I was the only one in Florida. This was not what I planned when I moved to Captiva.

John and I took Mom back to the house, and on the way I asked her about driving and the accident. At first, she denied everything, until John told her it was all right. Eventually she admitted she was driving, but she insisted a car nearly hit her and turned into the tree by accident. When I asked her about her vision, she said she didn't want to discuss it, she was fine.

Mom stood in the hallway looking at the new carpet and paint. True to form, she said the carpet was wrong, and she was sure the color of paint drying on the walls was not what she had chosen. After getting her normal criticism out of the way, she admitted the place looked much better and smelled fresh and clean. In her bedroom, she had a hard time accepting that I had thrown out the old bedclothes, but she said my father would probably like the new bedspreads.

I spent the evening with John and Caroline before driving back to Captiva. I told John I had to go into work in the morning, but I would see him and Mom at the hospital or at the house later in the afternoon. John said that was 'fine,' but before I left, he reminded me he was leaving on Saturday. Driving home, I talked through the situation out loud. In the end, I concluded in the short term I would have to live with my mom in Naples or she would have to live with me in Captiva. Both options seemed impossible.

Crossing the short bridge into Captiva I began to relax, the worries about my dysfunctional family replaced by glimpses of the beach and water. I pulled into my drive with the headlight off. There was a light on in the front room that was on a timer. Pulling up to the house, I had the impression of shadows moving in the kitchen. Stopping the car, I opened the glove box and took out a loaded Walther. I was tired and I knew I might be imagining the shadows, but there was no reason to take chances.

Walking around to the front of the house, I peeked in the front windows, but saw nothing. At a moment like this, I wished I had a basement. Entering either the front or back door meant disarming the alarm system or setting off the alarm. If I set off the alarm, the police should call in three minutes and I was to give them a password. If not, the troops would start arriving. The problem was if someone was in the house, he must have disarmed the alarm already.

I slipped my key in the door and quietly opened the front door with the gun leading the way. Lying in a chair was Saul Bernstein. He looked to be unconscious. There was dried blood on his face and shirt; he had taken a bad beating. Standing next to Saul with a knife against his throat was a short, hard muscled Hispanic man with a bandaged left hand and a scar on his face. Esteban Boca. I had surprised him.

"Senior Cederberg, we have been waiting for you. Now, please, I want you to lower your gun and put it on the floor. If you raise it, I will kill your friend."

"If you kill him I will shoot you. You only get one move in this game, and you have a knife and I have a gun."

"Si, but perhaps I'm willing to try." His free hand moved to his pants pocket. I assumed he had a pistol.

I pointed the Walther at him. "Keep your hand out of that pocket, and put the knife on the table, so we can talk."

"No, my knife stays where it is." He pushed the point against Saul's neck.

"Why you are here?" I asked.

"Where is the girl?"

"What girl?"

"Nina."

"Nina's dead. Your boss knows that. She died from an overdose."

"I hear otherwise. I hear the policeman took her. She isn't dead. She is hiding. Cracker Jack is hiding her and he knows where she is." He pointed to Saul. "But, he wouldn't talk."

"That's because as far as we know, Nina is dead. If you think Jack Jenson has her out in the swamp somewhere, then your beef is with Jack not me or Saul."

"Yes, but this one has been selling guns to the Indians. Guns they will use against us one day. The Don, he is very angry."

"You are lying. The Don didn't send you here. This is Andy's doing. You are Andy's errand boy. He sent you." Esteban said nothing, but his face was pure hatred.

"So what happens now?" I asked.

"You tell me where Nina is and I leave. Don't tell me and I kill him and then you." Esteban took his eyes off me and looked at Saul. I knew I could shoot Boca before he could move; the question was whether he would be able to put the blade in Saul. Even with a kill shot, sometimes a tough guy lasts a minute or two. A lot of time to act and this guy was tough.

"Esteban," I shouted, drawing his eyes to mine. "If you put your knife down now, I will let you leave here alive. I've a message for the Don. I want you to take it. Look at me," I shouted again, this time drawing his complete attention. "Set the knife down or die. This time he lowered his blade away from Saul's throat. If I was going to kill him, now was the time.

"How did you get here?"

"Truck."

"Are you alone? Is there anyone upstairs or waiting in the truck?"

"No I'm alone."

"What kind of truck?"

"A Chevy half ton."

"What color and year."

"Red, 1980."

"Okay. I want you to take a message back to Don Valdez. Not to Andy, but to the Don. I want you to tell him what you did here and what happened. Make sure he knows that I let you go. Tell him, I've nothing to do with this girl Nina. I have my own problems, and I do not need or want to be caught up in Andy and Nina's problems. Do you understand?"

"Of course."

"Okay, I'm going to give you twenty minutes to leave the island."

"What about him?" asked Esteban pointing to Saul.

"He has been beaten up before. Tell Don Valdez that all our gun sales to Immokalee are terminated. To him and to Jack. Tell him it is because of his family did not keep his word."

"He's not going to like that."

"I don't give a shit what he likes. This isn't any way to conduct business and he will know that. Tell him if he wants to reestablish our business ties, he can contact me at the club. You got that?"

"Yes."

"Okay, Esteban, set the knife on the table and slide it over to me. He did.

"Now put your hands on the table and assume the position. I'm going frisk you before I let you go."

"Fuck you, he said, but when I pointed the gun at his head, he placed his hand on the table and spread his legs. With the gun on his head, I use my other hand to do a quick frisk. In his right pocket was a revolver, which I pulled out. Then, before he could react, I slammed the butt of the Walther down with his right index finger and hand. As he turned, I pistol whipped him and knocked him to the ground, kicking him for effect.

"I couldn't let you do that to my friend and leave you unscratched. If I ever see you again, I will kill you. I'd like to kill you now, but you aren't worth the hassle. If there is a next time, it will be different. Do you understand?"

"Yes," he said, holding his right hand with his bandaged left hand.

"Then get out of here and do it fast."

Esteban barged out the back door and started running. I watched him run, careful, he did not stop or turn back. After waiting to be sure he was gone, I carried a still unconscious Saul fireman style out to my truck. Lee Memorial was twenty minutes away. Half way there, Saul moaned and opened his eyes. At the emergency room, they treated him for a broken rib and for a possible fractured jaw. I was told, the next day they would have to perform surgery on his jaw. When asked what happened, I explained he was in a personal fight over a woman. I could tell the admitting nurse wanted to call the police, but the doctor looked at me, and said no, let's just find Mister Bernstein a room. It was five in the morning by the time I reach my house.

I spent the morning making calls. I started with George at the Club to warn him about Boca and Andy Valdez. Before getting off the phone, I made George promise he would wear the special Kevlar vests I had purchased with the Club's logo. Next I called the Lee Memorial to check on Saul. The nurse said he was doing well, but wouldn't say more.

My mom answered on the second ring. She said John was at Publics buying her groceries. When I asked her how she was doing, she said it was nice having John visit, but she missed dad. When I asked about Dad, she said the doctor wanted to meet at two thirty today to discuss, options. If John had been there I would have asked more questions, instead I just said I would see her at the hospital. Finished with family matters, I called Jack's in Immokalee. After waiting several minutes, Jack Jenson came on the line.

"Mister Jenson, Robert Cederberg here."

"Robert what can I do for you?"

"I had a visit from Esteban Boca. He seems to think that Nina is still alive. He roughed up Saul trying to finding out where she is?"

"I'm sorry to hear that."

"I notice you didn't deny Nina is alive."

"So."

"So if Nina is really on the reservation, then Boca is going to come at you or drive out to that Chickee hut to and find Nina."

"How would he find it?"

"You took me there once and I could find it. There have to be plenty of people who know that spot. If Nina is out there, she might be in danger right now."

"I wouldn't worry about that."

"Good, I won't. But here's the deal."

"I'm listening."

"I'm dealing with some family matters, my parents were in an accident,"

"I'm sorry to hear that."

"Yeah, well, it's complicated, and it requires my full attention."

"Families are like that. So what can I do?"

"If you get a chance, you could talk to Don Valdez for me. Tell him I've nothing to do with this, that I want nothing to do with this. All I want to do is help my parents and run my business."

"Time to be the good son."

"Something like that. Anyway, if you would tell Don Valdez I let Boca live because I didn't want any complications right now. Make sure he understands leaving him alive was a gift. If I see Andy or any of his crew again, there will be blood.

"I understand. But, I can't guarantee that Frank will even talk to me. We have our own thing going on, but I will try."

"I owe you," I said, feeling the old man wanted to say more.

"No, I owe you and Saul," he said before hanging up.

HOSPITAL VISITS

Chapter 7

Driving to the Club it struck me that John was leaving tomorrow and I had no plan. George made me put on my logo vest when I arrived and then over instant coffee we went through the bills and talked about the appointment schedule. Without Saul, we would have to juggle the appointments between the two of us. Talking it through, we agreed I needed to be in Naples. George suggested we move my appointments to the mornings and then I could go to Naples to be with my mom and brothers in the afternoon. Knowing that we were meeting with Dad's doctor that afternoon, I left everything to George to arrange.

We met in the Neurosurgeon's office at two in the afternoon, it was a Friday. Caroline appeared very anxious. John said very little. Dad's doctor was a man in his forties.   A tall man he had on a white lab coat over an expensive suit. After a few introductory remarks, he jumped right in.

"We need to perform surgery on your husband. We need to fuse his spine." Using a model, he explained how the surgery would require screwing this device on Dad's head. It would keep his neck and head aligned for the three months recovery. At the mention of a three-month recovery, I asked the doctor whether my dad would be in the hospital for three months.

"No, he will be here for two weeks, and then he will have to move to a rehabilitation facility. Ultimately, he will probably have to live in a nursing home."

"Nursing home!" I repeated.

"When will he come home?" Caroline asked.

"If you can arrange home nursing care he might live at home, but most families can't provide what is required. Patients with this type of injury end up in nursing care."

"Who will pay for that?" asked John.

"Your father's health care will cover the surgery and first sixty days or so of nursing care. After that, either you pay, or you have to qualify him for Medicaid."

"He has Medicare. We both do." said my mother.

"Actually, they are different. I suggest you talk to a lawyer or the benefits person in the hospital. Regardless, he needs the surgery."

"What if he doesn't get it," I asked.

"He might never leave the hospital. Mrs. Cederberg, your husband needs this surgery. Do I have your approval?"

"Of course," my mother said.

"Good, I've scheduled the surgery for tomorrow morning."

"On Saturday" I heard you never want to have surgery done on the weekend," I said in desperation.

"That is a myth. Your dad will go in at eight, and be out by noon."

"Noon, that long?" said John.

"This is major surgery."

We spent a few minutes asking additional questions, and then the doctor ushered us out, saying he would see us tomorrow. Before going home, we spent an hour with Bill sitting in an activity room. Bill looked better and acted like the brother I knew. He was joking and flirting with the nurses. When I asked him about the therapy sessions, he said, "They are bullshit, but I have to attend and participate to get out. The good thing is I'm not the worst case in the group. We have hard-core drug addicts and long-term drunks. Guys who have lost their home and family. All this sprinkled with teenage glue huffers."

"Sounds like a real group of winners," said John.

"Well, there are a few losers, but there are a few who are trying. There is this girl, she is a junkie, heroin and cocaine, but she is trying. Besides, she is a babe. She has been here for a while. When she gets out, I'm going to get her phone number.

"What did you say?" I said.

"I'm going to get her number."

"What is her name?"

"Nina," he said.

Perfect, I thought. The cop in Immokalee, Burton, takes Nina to the drug unit in Naples. He has her locked up for her own safety. And, then he issues a false death announcement. In Naples, she can get clean of drugs and Andy Valdez. Hiding in plain sight.

"Bill, is this girl in her twenties, short dark hair, looks like she might be an American Indian?"

109

"She does have dark skin, but in Florida who knows. Don't tell me you know her."

"I think she might be my girl on the beach?"

"What girl on the beach?"

"The one I saved."

"Robert, what are you talking about?"

"Never mind, the less you know the safer you are."

"Robert, what the hell are you talking about?" asked John.

"Saul and I know this girl. We met by accident. Her boyfriend is a drug dealer. She overdosed. He was told she died, but he has gotten wind she is alive. He sent a guy to talk to me, but Saul got in the way and took a beating. I think if the boyfriend finds this girl he might kill her."

"Now I get why she doesn't talk in group."

"Robert, we don't need to hear about your criminal friends. This is what comes from owning a gun store," said Caroline, looking annoyed.

"Gun Club, mom. A Gun Club."

"Never mind. I need some dinner. Bill, I want you to stay away from this Nina girl."

"I have to agree with that," I added. "She is trouble." Looking at Bill, I wondered if I had just thrown down the gauntlet. He had that look he'd get when he was determined to drink and drive just to defy you.

"Seriously Bill. Helping his girl is dangerous."

"You don't seem afraid."

110

"Last night I came within an inch of shooting the man who broke into my house looking for this girl."

"What stopped you?"

"I've enough going on with Mom and Dad."

"And, me."

"And, you. If I had shot the man I would have spent all night with the police."

"Did you call the police?"

"No."

"Why not?" asked Bill.

"I just didn't need the hassle."

"Is that the only thing that kept you from shooting him, the hassle?" asked John. I could tell that he expected an answer and that he could not handle the truth. I was John's older brother. I was a success. I lived on the beach and had my own business. We never talked about the war or what happened in Michigan or here. The fact that the family had a killer in its midst had never been a topic for Thanksgiving. Now was not the time.

"Bill, when will you be discharged?" I asked.

"I'm being evaluated on Monday."

"Well, I know Mom could use your help, but I think you should take all the time you need to sort things out."

"What are you saying Robert?"

"I'm saying if another week or two of therapy helps you get on the road to recovery, then you should take it. The last thing Mom needs is to have to take care of you too."

"Don't you mean the last thing you want?" Bill shouted.

"Billy, take it easy," said John, before I could answer. "Don't mind Robert, you know how he is. You need to focus on getting out of here and helping mom. That means staying off the drugs."

"John, not you too!"

"Billy, Robert might be a cold hearted bastard, but he is right. Mom and Dad are going to need all of us, including Austin. They can't take care of themselves anymore. It will be up to us."

I wanted to react to the word 'anymore,' but there was no point. Bill and John shared a view of the world that was their own and had little to do with Austin or me. They grew up with a different Mom and Dad from mine. For Bill, his Mom and Dad were the parents who weren't there for him, as he got older. In high school, he started smoking marijuana and drinking beer and Mom and Dad acted as if they were unaware. I suppose the same is true for me, but I grew up during the time when they were trying harder to be parents. For me, they were too confining and I had to hide everything from them. For Bill I suspect it was just the opposite. They let him run wild.

Back at the house, Caroline watched TV, while John and I made a simple dinner, hamburgers and green salad. After dinner, Caroline went to bed, leaving us to talk.

Once we were alone, I asked John, "Are you still planning to leave in the morning? I assumed with dad's surgery, he would stay, but I had not asked.

"I'm not sure. If he doesn't make it, I will have to come right back. If the surgery goes well, then there is nothing I can do for Dad for a couple of weeks."

"Is that how you think of this, week by week?"

"How should I think about it? Day to day?"

"No, we need a permanent solution."

"Like what?"

"Look, Dad is never coming home. He is going into a nursing home. That leaves Mom on her own."

"She can't take care of herself."

"We don't know that. Dad never let her."

"If she was in an adult community she might be fine."

"Do you know of someplace?"

"I was thinking of one in Michigan."

"You mean move Dad and her?"

"I not sure what I mean, John. Do you think you can get your work to give you another week off?"

"Why, what good will that do?"

"Perhaps we should get Austin to come down and the four of us can discuss this together with mom."

"What are we discussing?"

"Where Mom and Dad will live and who will take care of them."

"There is nothing to discuss. They live here."

"And, you think I will take care of them?"

"Why not?"

"Where do I start? Look, if Dad dies, I think Mom should move back to Michigan.

"You think that is what she wants?"

"Honestly, I've never asked."

"Let's start there."

We stayed up late talking and drinking. I can't remember the last time we talked so much and so honestly. John is a decent guy and a good brother. The problem is I wanted to go back to Captiva and he wanted to go home to Michigan. Being honest, neither of us wanted to take care of our mom and dad. When John asked about Nina, I explained what had happened, but I could tell he did not understand. Why did I involve myself with such a girl and why did I know people like Boca or Andy Valdez. I didn't bother to point out Bill probably knew similar people. John lived a normal existence and I lived on the edge.

The next morning, we arrived late and Dad was already in surgery when we reach the surgical waiting room. Mom spent the morning praying and asking would he be alright. Robert went outside to drink coffee and sit on a bench in the sun.

For a while, I paced in the waiting room and then I went up to see Bill. For whatever reason, he was having a bad morning, and after five minutes of talk about dad, he asked me to leave, claiming he wanted to sleep. I wasn't sure if he was bothered by the fact he couldn't get out and be with Dad or even see dad.

On my way out, I stopped at the nurses' station and asked about Nina. I said I knew she used Grace and Tiger as last names, but I wasn't sure what name she might be using here.

"I'm assuming you are not family."

"No, I don't really know her, but I tried to help a girl who I thought was committing suicide and when my brother described this girl in his group I wondered if it was her? All I want to do is see how she is."

After looking me up and down, the nurse said, "You might check in the activity room."

"Thanks."

"By the way, someone else was asking about her."

"Do you remember what he looked like?"

"Mexican. Dark features, scar on his face. I told him the usual, we do not give out patient information, but then I told him we didn't have a patient like he described."

"Did he believe you?" I asked.

"I'm not sure, but he gave me a hard look."

"Why did you tell me?"

"I know your brother. He has talked a lot about you. For what it is worth, that girl is trouble. Both you and your baby brother should stay away from her," she said.

"Probably great advice, anything else."

"Oh yeah, the Mexican had two bandaged hands, if that helps."

"It does actually, and you were right to not tell him about Nina. If I were you, I might call that policeman who brought Nina in and tell him Esteban Boca was here. That's Boca."

"Thanks, I will."

"Good luck."

The activity room had four or five patients sitting at tables playing cards or reading. The room was bright with four south facing windows. There was a radio playing the Wave, with its mix of pop and oldies. I saw Nina before she saw me. I'm not sure she knew who I was. After all, we only met for ten minutes at night.

"You're the guy with the house, the guy on the beach. Your brother is in here on a thirty day."

"We are hoping he can get out sooner," I said. "What about you? I heard you OD."

"Yeah, Tom Burton saved me."

"Officer Burton."

"Tommy and I go way back. We knew each other in high school before Andy."

"He brought you here to hide you."

"He brought me here to get clean. He's hoping Andy will think I'm dead."

"When you get out, will you go back?"

"No, if I show my face in Immokalee, Andy will never leave me alone.   He might even hurt me." She spoke without any emotion or fear. She looked directly at me, watching my reaction.

"Why?"

"After the deal at your house, I knew I had to get out. I had to get away from Andy. The problem was I needed money, so I went into Andy's stash and stole some product. Not much, maybe a thousand dollars' worth, but Andy caught me. He sent Esteban with a message."

"Did he hurt you before giving you the overdose?"

"I don't want to talk about it."

"How about Jack Jenson. Does he know you are here?"

"Why would I tell him anything?"

"I had the impression you might be related. Like a granddaughter or something."

"He says that, but there is no proof. Don't get me wrong. It is possible we are related. I lived with him and Clara when I was in high school. They were really good to me."

"So when do you get out of here?"

"In four days. I think."

"What will you do?"

"Run, I guess."

"If I give you money to get out, will it just go back in your arm?"

"I hope not. I'm clean and want to stay that way, but I've said that before."

"Do you have family in Florida?"

"No. It is just me. What if I come and stay with you. I can tell you want me and I like you. We could have fun together. I'm even a good cook," she offered.

"If you had asked me that a week ago, I might have taken the chance, but right now I can't. I've too much going on. My family has to come first. My brother."

"I understand you don't owe me anything."

"Look, I have to go check on my dad, he is in surgery. Let's talk tomorrow or Monday. I'll see what I can do to get you safely out of here with enough money to start again. Maybe in six months or a year, we can get together. That will be up to you. What do you say?"

"Go check on your dad. I'll be here." She leaned in and kissed my cheek. She smelled good and looked even better.

On my way down the stairs, I heard my name called over the PA. Running back to the surgical waiting room, I was confronted with my mother crying in a chair and John hugging her.

"Robert, where have you been? It's your father," screamed my mother.

"What happened?"

"The doctor was just out, Dad died in surgery, said John. "Where were you?" he added.

"I was with Bill."

"You sit with Mom, I'll call Austin and then go tell Bill," said John to me before I could say anything more.

~*~

Austin flew down alone for the funeral. Bill got out early so he could be at the service. When I picked Bill up, I spent a few minutes with Nina. I wanted to spend more, and I considered the idea of her staying with me on Captiva. For a reason I could not explain. I wanted to protect her. I wanted to give her shelter and help her start a new life. You might say I was in love with her, except, I'm not sure I've ever been in love, and we had never even kissed. In the end, I gave her two thousand dollars, a ticket to Detroit, and the name of my lawyer Bruce Cabot.

FRESH STARTS

Chapter 8

Bruce was in his Grosse Pointe office when I called. I pictured him wearing a gray suit and drinking coffee out of his "World's Greatest Lawyer" mug.

"Bruce, Robert Cederberg."

"Robert, long time. How are you?"

With considerable difficulty and after many lawyer questions, I explained about my dad, my family, Nina, and the danger I might be sending Bruce's way. Being Bruce, he said, let's take things one-step at a time and worry about Nina if she shows up. His immediate concern was how to help untangle my mom from the financial situation in which she now found herself. Getting off the phone, I was grateful for a friend like Bruce.

A week later, he called me and started by saying "I broke one of my own rules."

"Which rule is that Bruce," I asked laughing.

"The rule against taking a woman client to lunch and not telling my wife?"

"So Nina showed up. What is she going to do?"

"I arranged for her to stay in an apartment near the Hill. I have a client who owns a Fourplex. I told him she was using an alias to evade her abusive husband. She chose the name Grace May."

"That is pretty close to her real name."

"I know, but I think it is safe. It would take a very good detective to make the connection. Now, I'm trying to get her a job in retail. I've a friend at Jacobson. That might be harder because they will want a real social security card. We will see."

"What do you think? Was she clean when you saw her?"

"I think so, but only time will tell. She certainly is beautiful."

"I know."

"Want her address and phone number? I think she would like to thank you."

"Not right now, maybe later. Now I need a different favor."

I explained that in going over my parents accounts, we had questions about my dad's debts and selling the house. Before I got very far, Bruce was mapping it out for me. He licensed to practice in Florida, and because of several clients, he was very familiar with probate and bankruptcy law in Florida. After an hour on the phone, he said, "Why don't I lay out what you need to do, and when you are ready, I will come down for a few days and take care of it all, provided I can stay with you on Captiva. That way I can file all the paper work and still get in a little golf."

"Put together what we need to do and let me know when you want to come down. And, make sure you bill me for everything."

"Everything?"

"Well, not lunch."

"Okay."

~*~

"Anything on the schedule," I asked when I arrived at the Club. Saul was working behind the counter. His wired jaw appeared to be a boom in sales. Customers would ask what happened and when he explained how he fought off an intruder, they would buy extra ammo.

"You have a handgun safety class at ten and Jack Jenson called and asked if we could talk with him around eleven. Said he was coming in with the misses for some shopping at the new Edison Mall."

"What do you think he wants?"

"I don't know, but I don't think it can be good."

"I'll be in back. Call me when he comes in."

"Should I call George or have Eddie come in?" Eddie was our clean up boy.

"No, if it was Andy Valdez, I'd say call George, but we should be okay with Jack."

Jack arrived alone around eleven fifteen. He had dropped his wife and a daughter at the mall. Today he looked like a classic Florida Cracker on vacation. He had on a White floppy hat, a brown Izod shirt with green stripes, tan slacks, and white loafers. If he had been wearing a white belt, he would have been the full Cleveland.

"Jack," I said. "You are looking good. How can we help you?"

"Robert, might we talk in your office?"

"Of course, should Saul be with us?" The old man considered Saul for a moment.

"Saul more than anyone," he said.

I placed a sign on the lobby counter next to a bell that said ring for service and we retreated to the office. I got Jack a coffee, and let him proceed at his own pace.

"Robert, when you told me what happened at your house, you left me with the impression that you let that varmint Boca go so he could take a message back to Frank Valdez. The message being you had no idea about Nina being alive, and you didn't know where she is, if she was alive."

"That is about the gist of it," I said. "Esteban was lucky I had other problems on my mind, because all I did was bust up his hand."

"Yes, I was sorry to hear about your father. As for Esteban, someone needs to take him out to the swamp."

"Well, Saul and I still owe him a visit."

"Call me when that happens. Right now, my problem is Tom Burton. He seems to think you helped Nina leave Florida and now only you know where she is."

"What if I did?"

"Well, Tom was planning to take her away. He's been in love with that girl since she was fifteen. Only, thing is, she left the hospital early. She told her doctor she wanted to escape both Tom and Andy."

"Good for her."

"Yes, I might feel that way too, except for Tom. See to begin with Tom is a cop and that gives him certain access and liberties you and I don't have. Tom is a plodder, but he can be a hound dog, too. Right now, Tom is trying to find Nina. When the doctors told him she was gone, he went after Andy, got him alone, and busted him up some. Enough that he realized Andy knows nothing. Except now, Andy knows everything Tom knew. He knows she is alive and was in Naples Hospital. Apparently, Tom got to the doctor who took care of Nina first, and he pressured him into telling what he knew. He told Tom she said she was leaving Florida."

"Does Andy know this too?"

"I assumed he does, because the doctor is still walking around."

"So why tell me?"

"Because you gave her the money and bought her the airplane ticket, and now you have a friend helping her." Jack had the facts so right I doubted he was guessing.

"Who told you all that."

"Nina of course."

"She called you?"

"Two nights ago. She is lonely. She talked about you. Robert, as much as Nina has been through and seen, she is still a young girl. You are her knight."

"Except I'm not."

"Maybe."

"So what happened to Tom and Andy?"

"Tom has been to see me twice and back to the doctor in Naples. He is following leads. Eventually, he will learn about your brother Bill being on the same unit. He will learn you saw Nina, and when he does, you will be his next stop.

"What about Andy?"

"Andy has disappeared."

"You mean Tom killed him?"

"No, I think he knows she is in Michigan and he is on his way to Michigan to find Nina."

"How would he find that out?"

"Same way I did."

"Oh no. You think she called Andy."

"That girl has been in love with Andy since she was seventeen, but more than that, she can't be alone."

"Is Andy flying there?"

"No, driving with Boca and his crew."

"Why would he do that?"

"Because it is hard to take machine guns on airplanes."

"Jesus. Are you sure about this?"

"I talked to Don Valdez yesterday. That is why I'm here. Frank said Andy called from Daytona. He asked Frank for a contact in Detroit. Somehow, he traced her to there, but he did not get it from me. Nina didn't tell me where she is and she didn't give me her phone number."

"But Tom could have easily learned both."

"I think he has. He called me this morning and asked if I knew anyone in Michigan, in Detroit who might be helping Nina."

"Of course I could honestly tell him no, but he had her phone number.

"Then he has an address."

"No, that's what is interesting. Nina is smarter than I would have guessed. Tom said she used a pay phone."

"What do you want me to do?"

"If you know where she is or how to reach her, call her and give her a heads up. She isn't safe where she is."

"What should I tell her to do?"

"I think she should buy a car and drive back down to Florida. If she will stay clean and sober, I can arrange for her to hide on one of the reservations."

"And then what?"

"Then I wait for Andy to return and we take him into the swamp."

"What about Tom."

"One problem at a time. My guess is Nina can handle Tom if Andy was out of the picture. She has before." The old man looked down at the floppy white hat in his hands

"Jack, I hate to say this, we might be expecting too much from a girl who was on a Psych unit only a week ago. Maybe we should just warn her and let her figure out her next move. If you get involved you will have a war. Is that what you want really? Is Nina worth it?"

"She is family."

"She said she wasn't"

"I know, what she thinks, but she is my niece. My youngest sister gave her up in nineteen sixty when she was a baby. If she had come to me back then, I could have raised her right. However, she came to me when she was fifteen, and wild. Too late." He sighed and looked down for a moment. For the first time, I thought Jack might be lying or hiding something. Nina was running from him as much as any of the others. Taking a moment, I looked at Saul.

"What do you think Saul?"

"I'm not so sure about this cop, this guy Tom. He is a loose cannon. On the other hand, when you decide to take Andy and his friends into the swamp, I hope you will call me."

"You can count on it."

"So what do you say Robert? Can you get a hold of Nina?"

"Honestly, I'm not sure. She will have to call me. I don't know where she is or how to find her. But, I will let you know if I talk to her."

"I guess that is all we can do. Now, before I leave, how about selling me some ammo? I've a list."

~*~

I was waiting at the baggage claim in Ft. Myers when Bruce Cabot and Nina emerged. Nina ran up to me and hugged me putting her arm through mine. Disengaging myself, I shook Bruce's hand

128

and helped him grab bags. Bruce was dressed in suit pants, a polo shirt and black tassel loafers. In the three years since I had seen him, his hair looked thinner with more gray. Shaking hands, I remembered how solid and dependable Bruce could be. I was glad I had called him.

Nina wore tight black jeans and a short-sleeved turtleneck, with her short black hair, high cheekbones, and dark eyes; she looked like Audrey Hepburn playing an Indian princess. Driving to Captiva, Nina talked mostly about Grosse Pointe and Detroit.

Pulling into the back drive, I checked out the house before letting Bruce and Nina into the house. At the second floor stairway, Bruce asked me where he should put his bags, and I realized I had no plan for where they would sleep. Trying to be practical, I said Bruce could use my room and after suggesting lunch at the Duck and then a walk on the beach, I pointed Nina to the guess room to change into shorts and her bathing suits. In my plan, I would sleep on the sleeper couch in the second bedroom. However, Bruce and Nina decided otherwise, he took the guest room after Nina put her bag in the master.

Lunch at the Duck was fun, Bruce and I both teased and flirted with Nina. For an hour, we avoided any more talk about Tom, Andy, or Jack. After lunch, we walked for twenty minutes and then sat without talking, just absorbing energy from the sun. Before walking home, we wadded out and swam in the ocean. Eventually, I led them back to the house where Bruce retreated to the guest room for a nap, and I began a new chapter.

In your life, certain things, events, seem inevitable. When I met Nina on the beach and she looked at me with that help me look, I knew I was lost. For many men, the woman who they should marry is the woman who loves them, meaning regardless of how many women the man sleeps with, has great sex with, and is attracted to. The right woman is that one woman who is willing to put up with all his foibles. Unfortunately, many men fall in sex with a woman who stokes their libido but little else.

For me, there have been so few women in my life, I start with the woman who seem most attracted to me. In Nina case, I wasn't sure who wanted the other more. That afternoon locked away, safe in my house, the sex was good, but not great, it was as if we were hesitant to commit. It was like each of us wasn't ready to take the gloves off, we were sparing, testing each other. Thinking about the difference between Nina and some of my other beach friends, most of the women I meet on the beach are looking for sex and I am happy to participate, but they were not looking for me. With Nina, it felt like she was looking for me.

Lying back, I grabbed several pillows from the floor and propped them behind her head and mine. "What do you think?" I asked, not knowing what else to say.

"We can work on it. This isn't about sex, it never was," she said.

"What is it about?"

"You and I need each other. We aren't normal. We are missing a piece. When you called me out of the surf, I was going to kill myself, I had given up. You gave me hope."

"Is that what you were missing, hope?"

"Fucking right. Every addict has lost hope. I felt like I was living on borrowed time. Everyone around me only cared about what I could do for them or what they could do to me. I was an object, a source of income, a fuck. You are different. You don't look at me that way."

"Neither does Bruce."

"Well, Bruce is married. He loves his wife. He looks at my body, and he has thoughts about it. But even, Bruce, as nice as he is, doesn't look at me the way you do."

"When I look at you I see a beautiful girl who needs help. How is that different from Bruce?"

"Because when you look at me, you give me hope."

"I give you hope."

"You look at me, and I feel like a real person again. I feel safe and new." She gave me a hug before walking off to the bathroom.

Yes, but for how long? I thought.

~*~

In the morning, I called my mom's house and talked to Austin. Two hours later, Bruce, Saul, George, and I were sitting with my brothers Austin, John and Bill in the Club's member room. Austin had convinced Mom that this was a brothers only meeting, just as I had insisted that Nina stay in Captiva with the alarm set.

131

Sitting in the middle between my real brothers and my partners and my lawyer, I felt a real sense of safety. These six men were the only people I could trust. Men, with whom I could be honest.

"To start," I said, "I want it clear, no one is being asked to do anything illegal. I find myself in a bind, and before I act, I want your advice, your counsel. From now on, whatever I do, I want your honest opinion."

"Go ahead," said Bill.

"First, Nina the girl from Bill's therapy group is staying with me on Captiva. I arranged for Nina to go to Michigan, where Bruce was helping her, but Michigan became too dangerous. Bruce and Nina flew down here yesterday."

"I thought this meeting was about Mom," said Austin.

"Austin," Bill said, putting his hand on his shoulder, "let Robert talk."

"Nina has a checkered past. She is on the run from her ex-boyfriend, a really bad player, with local drug connections. He has a crew of three bodyguards. One man, Esteban Boca beat up Saul. He is very dangerous. He gave Nina the overdose that sent her into Naples hospital." I saw that Austin was looking at around the room. He stopped and looked at John for understanding.

"I am telling you this because I've promised to keep Nina safe"

"What about the police?" asked Austin.

132

"Men like Andy and Boca are outside of the law. To get at me they might go after Mom or any of you. Boca attacked Saul simply because he knew me." I looked at Saul.

"Does this Andy know Nina's with you on Captiva?" asked John.

"I don't think so, but he will. For all I know, my house and the Bullseye are being watched"

"What about Jack Jensen?" asked Saul.

"Who is he?" asked Bill.

"Jack Jenson is a bar owner in Immokalee. He claims to be Nina Uncle. She worked in the bar. I'm not sure whether he is an ally or another threat. He and Nina are part Seminole. He wants her to hide on the reservation. He says she will be safe there, but she says no. I don't know what to believe. Whatever else, he is a player."

"So, what are you going to do? How will you keep her safe?" asked George.

"Let's look at the options starting with the goal," said Bruce, standing up to take charge of the conversation.

"The goal is to make it safe for Nina and Robert," said Saul.

"And Mom," said Bill.

"The goal is to make it safe for Nina and Robert to be together without any harm coming to the people in this room and your families," said Bruce summarizing.

"You don't really think my family in Detroit is in danger?" demanded Austin.

"Whatever happens, no one will be safe with Boca alive," said Saul. "I spent time with that guy, we drank beer together and I can tell you he is one dark motherfucker. One minute we are shooting guns together, the next he has a knife at my throat and is beating the shit out of me." Saul rubbed his jaw. "That fucker has to go."

"What are we talking about?" shouted John. "Are you planning a murder?"

"No, or course not, I said, trying to assure myself. "No one has to kill Boca or Andy. We just have to neutralize Boca and Andy." I said.

"What about putting them in jail?" asked John.

"Jail might be enough, but they could always arrange for a hit on Robert," said Bruce.

"Or any of us," said George.

"If Andy and Boca are taken out, what will Don Valdez do?" asked Saul, not putting too fine a point on his words.

"The Don might stand for Boca, but never Andy. If he thinks we had anything to do with an attack on Andy, the Don will come at me."

"How can we neutralize Andy and take out Boca without getting the Don on our case?"

"This is why we have the police." Shouted Austin, trying to get his point heard.

"What about the police?" asked Bill.

"Tom Burton might do something, if Nina asked. Unfortunately, she will never act against Andy. She knows he is bad for her, but I think she loves him still."

"Then why is she with you?" asked John.

"I offered her a safe haven. Oh, she cares for me. She may even like me. But, it isn't love, regardless of what she says." This was the first time I had admitted what I was feeling and it caused me to wonder what I was doing placing everyone in danger for a girl who didn't really love me.

"Robert. I hate to say this, but this girl is dangerous. She has you wrapped around her finger. She says she is in love with you, and you want to believe her." Bruce wiped sweat from his forehead.

"The trouble is if these men learn she is with you, they will come at you with everything they have. Too much perhaps to fight, but even if you win, what will you have? More bodies and more to explain to the police."

"What do you suggest, Bruce."

"Go to the police now. Tell them the story. Let Nina testify that Boca gave her an overdose. Make them give her protection. Start using the system, before you have to kill someone else. Unless…"

"Unless what Bruce?"

"Robert, I don't think we want to go into this here."

"Bruce, we are all brothers here. Say what's on your mind."

"Robert, I worry about you. I think we all do. I worry that you want this confrontation. You want to kill these men. Maybe you miss the war. I don't know, I'm not a doctor, but the idea of killing them doesn't bother you."

"It doesn't bother me either Counselor," said Saul.

"Yes, I'm aware of that. What about you George?"

"No, I'm bothered by the idea, but if there is no alternative, I'm prepared to kill. I once shot a man from a mile away. I watched his head explode in my scope. There is nothing more personal, unless it is putting your hand over a man's mouth and jamming a knife between his ribs."

"I'm going back to Mom's," declared Austin. "I don't want to be any part of this.

"Me neither, " said John. "I've a wife and children. I'm here because our father just died and our mother needs our help. This girl is nothing to me. I have a job and a family. I wasn't in the Army. I protested against the war. I voted for McGovern and Jimmy Carter for God's sake. I'm not getting involved in some plot to kill some drug dealer and his henchman. This whole discussion is wrong. You need to go to the police. If this girl is in danger, it is her own doing. Let the police help her."

John stopped, gaining support from Austin. Taking my arm, he started to cry. "Robert, just when you were starting to act like a brother, you bring us into this mess." John looked at Bruce, but kept talking.

"Robert. You are my brother, and I want to help you because we are friends and brothers. The problem is, right now, I don't even know you. When are you going to act normal for a change?" When he finished, John slumped back in his chair exhausted.

"John, believe it or not, I'm glad you spoke up like this. I think you and Austin should take Mom and go back to Detroit and your families as soon as you can. Maybe tomorrow. I don't want you hurt, and I don't want you or Austin involved in any of this. Same goes for you Bill."

"But I want to help. I like Nina, and I know what she is going through. I can help, and I not afraid." said Bill.

"Honestly Bill, I could use your help with Nina and the drugs, but Bruce is right. Helping me will make you a target, and sooner or later I might have to kill Andy or Boca and if you help me, I am afraid we will both lose more of our connection to our family and to living a normal life."

"Whatever you do, you are going to have to find a place to hide Nina until this is over," said Bruce. "Someplace where she will be safe from Andy and Boca Someplace away from you Robert."

"Why away from me?"

"Because you are getting ready to stand out in the middle of a lightning storm."

"What's my alternative?"

"What if I talk to this Don Valdez for you," asked Bruce. "He is a business man. He will understand what is at stake."

"Lay the whole deal in front of him and ask him to intervene," said George. "You said he is a reasonable man."

"Yes, but what is in it for him?"

"He keeps his nephew."

Although I had my doubts, I said, "It might be worth a try."

COUNSEL

Chapter 9

A giant Hispanic man opened the door. His hands were twice as large as mine. "Don Valdez is having coffee on the patio. Please follow me," he said in Spanish flavored English. Our walk through the house reminded me of the Don's wealth and refinement.

The back patio was a cobblestone circle in a garden of roses and tropical plants. Hummingbird feeders hung at the borders of the garden. I noticed red-throated hummingbirds. Frank Valdez sat at an iron table with for four chairs. This morning his gray hair had been cut and looked bleaker. Like Bruce, Valdez was wearing light gray suit pants, a dress shirt, and a tie.

"Mister Cederberg. I did not think we would see each other this soon. And, this gentleman is your lawyer."

"Don Valdez, let me introduce Bruce Cabot. Bruce is visiting from Detroit. When I told him about a problem I had, he suggested we speak with you directly."

"Please have a seat. May I offer either of you coffee?" We both took chairs and accepted coffee from a white coated server. Don Valdez sat facing me, while Bruce spoke for me.

"Don Valdez. Mister Cederberg has a problem that he would like to solve without violence. A problem that involves your nephew Andy and your employee Esteban Boca."

"They are away at this time."

"Mister Cederberg sent a girl to me asking me to help her make a fresh start."

"You are talking about poor Nina. I understand she was in the hospital."

"According to Miss Grace, your son's bodyguard Esteban Boca gave her that overdose. Fortunately, Tom Burton saved her and got her into treatment in Naples. Sometime after that, this man Boca came to Mister Cederberg's house trying to learn where the girl was hiding. You may recall, Mister Cederberg agreed to stay out of Immokalee and your nephew Andy agreed to stay away from Captiva."

"Andy would not go against my word. I promise you Andy has not been on Captiva."

"Don Valdez, it was my understanding our agreement included Andy's body guards."

"Perhaps Esteban misunderstood. I will speak to both boys when they return."

"That is why we are here," I said. "We are hoping you will talk to these boys before there is more violence. Nina is back in Florida. She is trying to start a new life. Whatever she had with your nephew is over. If she owes him or you money, I will see the debt is repaid. Basically, I'm asking you to tell Andy and this man Boca to stay away from Captiva and to leave Nina alone."

"When they return, I will speak with Andy and Boca. If you have a problem with him, you will let me know."

"Don Valdez, if I have a problem with Andy or any of your men, I will assume your nephew does not respect your word and cannot be trusted. In which case the results could be fatal."

"What more would you have me do?"

"Perhaps you could send Andy away. Perhaps Andy could work for you in Mexico or Columbia for a while. I'm a firm believer that time and distance cures most things," said Bruce.

"I'm going to smoke a cigar, would either of you join me?" I signaled no, whereas Bruce accepted a Cuban cigar. For a while, the two men simply smoked as I watched the birds feeding in the garden.

"Robert, the last time you were here we talked about Don Quixote. After you left, I pick up my copy of Cervantes' two volumes in Spanish. Most people, if they know the story at all, know about Don Quixote charging at windmills on his shaky old horse. They know the funny stories in the first book. However, it is in the second book where Cervantes considers the nature of man. Don Quixote is cured of his madness and he no longer has a quest. Don Quixote suffers an illness that cures him of his madness. In the end, Don Quixote turns back into Don Alonso and dies."

"He might have been mad, but at least he was alive." I offered.

"Yes, I'm afraid that some men must tilt at windmills or die. I hope this will not be true for you. I hope you can return to your castle and live a happy life with your Dulcinea."

"That is all I'm asking."

"You have my promise, but don't forget there are others involved in this story, this policeman and Jack Jenson. I can't guarantee what they will do."

On the ride home, we talked about Don Valdez and whether we believed he could control Andy. As things stood, the bait was in the air and all I could do was wait.

Saul answered the back door with a loaded .38 caliber revolver.

"Where is Nina?" I asked.

"She is sitting on the beach with Bill. George is standing guard."

"Was that her idea?"

"She is anxious, nervous. I think she needs a drink."

"I'd rather she didn't drink. It is too easy to go back to drugs."

"So how did your meeting go?"

"Uncle Frank said all the right things, but I wasn't sure."

"What did you think Counselor?" asked Saul.

"He is very old school. A refined criminal," said Bruce, "but I'm unsure if he can control Andy or Boca. He is an old man. His power is no longer physical."

During the next week, Bruce returned to Detroit by plane. Austin and John loaded up John's car with Caroline's clothes and favorite possessions and returned to Michigan with Caroline in tow. According to Austin, she opted to stay at first with him, Susan, and Jake. In three months, she said she would either move into an apartment or move in with John. As for her house in Naples, she left that to Bill and me to sell. Bill had decided to stay at the house and work for me behind the counter in Ft. Myers.

"How was work," I asked over dinner.

"Hot," she answered. We were sitting on the front porch. Nina and I had settled into a simple pattern of life together. She moved her few belongings into my spare room. In the morning, we usually went for an early walk followed by a simple breakfast, coffee, toast, and juice. At first, Nina went with me and hung out at the club. In my spare time, I taught her to shoot. Eventually she got a job at a new store on the island, Chico's. The store was only three blocks from the house and she would walk to work or I would drive her before going to Ft. Myers. At night we made dinner together, we walked the beach, and then watched television or listened to music. Occasionally I would have a drink, she abstained. Most nights we slept together, but on nights when we argued or if she felt the need to be alone, then she slept in the guest room.

"The air conditioning stopped working. Then all these tourists showed up. Fat woman in tight fitting clothes. All trying to be young."

"I like the clothes on you," I said.

"I do too, but…" She looked away, out to the ocean.

"But what?"

"Selling clothes is so boring. I miss the night life."

"Selling booze to drunk Mexicans."

"I miss the dancing."

"You miss the attention."

"I miss the drinks and the tips."

"Shall we go out dancing?"

"You don't dance."

"You could dance for me; I have a pocketful of singles."

"Fuck you," she said, giving me the finger.

"That would be good too." I laughed, "It's been a while."

"Are you complaining?"

"No, not exactly, but it has been a while and I miss touching you and kissing you."

"I'm right here, she said. "We don't have to be in bed."

I reached out to touch her face, but she pulled away.

"Robert you are so predictable."

"Is that bad?"

"No, predictable can be good," she said, but I knew we were sleeping in different rooms again tonight.

Settling into a type of domestic life, didn't mean completely dropping my guard. I carried a gun wherever I went, and so did Nina. When we were in the house, the alarm was always set, and when we left, I was particularly vigilant. In my experience, the easiest way to take out a civilian target was when he was coming or going. Meaning, you watched his pattern of coming or going and planned to shoot him when he was distracted by locking the house or starting the car. The mafia liked to shoot a guy while he was eating. For a while, Saul, George, and I watched over Nina at work without telling her. We watched her from a block or more away as she walked back and forth, to and from work. Once she seemed safe, Saul and I went back to work, but George continued his surveillance on his off days.

It was on a Tuesday that George watched Nina go to lunch alone at the Bubble Room. Normally, Nina went home for lunch and when she ate out, she went with friends or she purchased a sandwich and soda form the deli next door and ate lunch on the beach. This day she was eating alone at an expensive tourist restaurant. Sitting across the street in his car, George saw Andy Valdez enter the restaurant ten minutes later. He was alone. Andy stayed for a half an hour and then left, driving off in a new Bronco. Five minutes later Nina walked home carrying a package. Minutes later, she went back to Chico's.

"What will you do?" George asked me over the phone.

"Find the package. Ask her about it."

"What about the lunch, will you ask her?"

"I'm not sure I want her or Andy to know we have been watching. It was obvious he was here to meet with Nina. My guess is she called him and either he came to Captiva against his Uncles orders or Andy and Uncle Frank are playing me."

"Don't forget about Nina."

"I haven't."

The package was easy to find. Nina put it in her suitcase in the guest closet. It was a simple white envelope tied with white string. Inside the envelope was a syringe kit, the type used by diabetics. Rather than wait for Nina I walked to Chico's. Seeing me, she ran to me and kissed me hello.

145

"How was your day," I asked.

"Slow, only a few customers."

"Nothing else?" I asked, giving her a hard look.

"You know, don't you? Have you been watching me?"

"No."

"You're lying, I can tell."

"What about you?"

"Look, okay. This is no big deal. Andy called at the store. He said he missed me. I was lonely. All he wanted was to meet me for lunch at the Bubble room. I wasn't in danger. No bodyguards, just Andy. He was the old Andy, sweet and fun. We shared a mushroom burger."

"What else did you share?"

"Fuck, you Robert. Andy wants me back. He says he loves me."

"Yea sure, he loves you so much he gave you a bag of dope and a syringe."

"So now you are going through my things."

"Actually, all I found the envelope with the needle. Where's the rest? Where's the Heroin or is it a speedball?"

"I told him I'm clean and mean to stay clear. I begged him to go into treatment, but Andy isn't ready... He's still using, but he will get there. I know he will."

"You realize whatever is in that bag will kill you. Andy is setting you up."

"Either that or the police are on their way to bust you and me."

"Andy wouldn't do that he loves me."

"You think he loves you, but then he sent Boca with an overdose."

"That was a mistake. Esteban was angry. He was jealous."

We had reached the back steps to the house.

"What do you mean, Esteban was jealous?"

"Esteban wanted me for himself, but I told him I couldn't do that to Andy. I loved Andy.

"Do you want to go back to Andy?" I asked, feeling I had lost her already.

"Do you want me to?"

"Of course I don't. I…"

"You what? You love me. You can't even say the words. I think you can never love anyone. You are too afraid of being vulnerable. You are still hiding in that shell you talk about. When we have sex, there is great intensity, but no passion. When Andy says he loves me, he means it. You just want to keep me safe. You carry your guns and say it is to protect me. What you really want is to kill. You miss it."

"No, you have it wrong. I've never said I love you because I don't know what that means. I care about you. I want to help you make a fresh start. I want to be your friend. To help you leave the drugs and Andy behind. I've never asked you to sleep in my bed. I want you to be with me because you want to. If you want to leave

147

and to go back to Andy, you should. If you stay clean and don't see Andy, you are welcome to stay here. If I see Andy, here in this house or on the island with you, there will be violence. He was warned. Andy has to learn there are consequences for not keeping his word." After my speech, Nina went to the guest room and I went for a walk. When I came back, she was still in the house. The next day she went to work, as if all was normal, but of course, everything had changed.

~*~

"So what are you going to do?" asked Saul.

"Wait, I guess."

"Too dangerous, said George.

"What if we arrange it so Andy kills Boca?" said Saul.

"Or better still, the two kill each other," offered George.

"Now, that is an interesting idea. How do we make that happen?" I asked.

"The usual suspects, said Saul, "jealousy, money, betrayal."

"I think we are past jealousy. They aren't going to fight over Nina."

"How could we make it look like Boca is stealing from Andy?" asked Bill.

"Better still, how about if both are caught stealing from Don Valdez," said George.

"That is a great idea," said Saul. "We know that Andy and his crew are collector drugs for the Family. What if we highjack a shipment they are supposed to collect and then we make it look like both of them are holding the goods."

"I like it, but those boys will be carrying machine guns. They aren't going to give up a shipment of drugs without a fight." I didn't bother to finish my thought.

"How about Jack Jensen and his Indian friends?" asked Saul.

"He isn't going to start a war, but he might be willing set up Andy."

"So how do we proceed?"

"We need some intelligence. We have to learn more about the Don's drug deliveries."

"I can take care of that," said George.

~*~

For the month of June, George and Saul divided their time following Andy. While they were on surveillance, Bill and I ran the Club. Working every day with Bill gave me a rare chance to get to know my brother as an adult. Sometimes we'd talk about Mom and Dad, and growing up in Grosse Pointe. In talking with Bill, I realized how much he loved both Eric and Caroline and yet how he still blamed them for his situation. When I asked him about needing drugs, he said he was doing okay. He said he was glad to be off of cocaine, but he missed the marijuana. I noticed he had stopped smoking and at Mom's house all he did when he went home was grilled a burger, drink a lot of ice tea, and watched TV.

"You need a girlfriend." I suggested one day at work.

"Unless she is a tea totter, I'm not ready yet. Dating means smoking and drinking. I couldn't talk to a woman without a drink."

"Well, be careful," I said. "Sooner or later, a Playboy just isn't enough."

At first, I worried about Bill living alone at Mom and Dad's house, but seeing him at the Club gave me hope. Bill was learning to shoot and sell. As a shooter, he was not a natural, but with practice, he started hitting the target. In terms of sales, he was nearly as good as George. He fits with customers, he dressed like our customers, he spoke their language, and he was a quick learner in terms of the features of each of the most popular guns. Whenever I worked in the back, I noticed that Bill would find a reason to come back and practice his shooting with me there to spot.

"You are getting better," I said one time after a good round.

"You and Saul are great teachers," he answered. I noticed Bill was still holding the pistol too tight, he wasn't relaxed; he was concentrating too hard, not a terrible trait. It meant he was slower, but accurate.

"All you need to do is relax," I said when we were back at the counter.

"I'm relaxed," he said, sitting on a stool behind the counter.

"I don't mean now, I mean when you are shooting. You are still gripping the gun too hard. Next time, you go to the range, just pick up the gun and shoot immediately. Don't aim and shoot. Just pick up the gun, point, and shoot. Just be careful you don't shoot your foot." I laughed.

"Thanks, I'll try that," he said, pretending to be a cowboy in a gunfight. Seeing him, I thought about playing shoot'em up with Bill and John as kids. Now it was real.

~*~

The flat, hard scrabble South Florida landscape made it was hard to find a high spot from which to watch the Valdez house. Across from the farm was a mile of open ground and cornfields. After a day of driving the back roads, George found a place off the road where he could drive in, hide the car, and then walk to within a mile of the villa without being seen. Going in early, he could watch the house from a mile away with a scope. On the second morning, he watched Andy drive off towards Immokalee and decided to follow into town.

"He was easy to find driving," said George. "He was driving that new Bronco. On Tuesday, I followed him to an apartment building in Immokalee. After twenty minutes, he came out with Boca. They drove to several other apartments around town. At each stop, they entered the apartment carrying a sports bag."

"Buying or Selling?" asked Saul.

"Could be both. Later, I followed them into the grasslands until they turned down a rutted track off Oil Well road. I couldn't risk being seen, so I drove on and walked back in. Ten minutes later a single engine private plane came in low and landed somewhere off the road. It was about five thirty. I didn't see the plane or any transfer, but I think we have found one of the collection points."

A week later, George followed Andy and Boca to a different spot off Oil Well road but again at dusk. The following week they went to the first drop off point. A week later, they went back to the second spot.

Knowing they would not be back to either spot for several days, Saul, George, and I drove to the first landing spot. Walking in on the road felt like being on patrol.

"Georgie, you ever miss the Marines," asked Saul.

"I don't miss the chow," said George.

"What about the action," I asked.

"What I miss is that moment when you take the shot and know it is a kill." He answered.

"I don't miss taking orders from some dumb ass Louie," said Saul.

"We have Robert for that."

"Please, I was a Sergeant."

"Close enough."

"What about you Robert. What do you miss?"

"Until I met Saul and you George, I missed the comradeship. Being brothers, with only one goal.

"To make it home," said George.

"To get laid," said Saul.

"Okay, two goals," I said.

"I remember this new guy," said Saul. "He came in with a group of replacements. He had been in Vietnam for three months working in an office in Saigon, and then they sent him and a bunch of other pencil necks out as replacements. His name was Ed Renickie. He was from Pittsburg. All he did was talk about home. All he wanted was to go home, drive his sixty-nine Camaro, and marry his girl. He had a picture of the two together. At first, no one listened to him and no one cared. Eventually the more days he survived, the more patrols he went on and came back from, the more I rooted for him. Eventually, all I wanted was for him to make it home, so I started watching out for him. I wanted him to make it. Hell, I wanted us all to make it. I stopped worrying about getting back myself and started watching out for Ed and the other guys. I can't explain it, but I think that saved me."

"What happened to Ed?"

"He stepped on a mine."

"What about the Camaro?"

"I thought about buying the Camaro when I got back."

"You thought about his girlfriend when you got back," added George.

"I did actually. Her and the car." We all laughed. Soldiers telling war stories. When we reached the end of the road, we easily found the landing strip. From a sniper point of view, there were plenty of places to hide and shoot, but jacking a bale of marijuana was another story. The road ended in a short strip of asphalt. It seemed like it would be impossible to get the jump on someone. The second spot was almost identical. According to George, a piper cub landed and dropped off two small bales of marijuana in exchange for a white package. The exchange took one minute and plane never

153

shut down the engine. After the plane taxied and took off, Boca and Andy loaded the bales in the Bronco and drove it to the Valdez farm. If we wanted to set Andy up for dealing, all we had to do was inform the police about one of the collection spots.

Once we knew where and when they collected their drug shipment, George came back to working in the store except for what we called 'collection day.' On those days George continued to watch Andy. On one collection day, Saul came out from the back carrying the extension phone. "George just called," he said. Andy and Boca are in the Ft Myers, Gateway getting gas. He says they are fifteen miles from the bridge. He's waiting by the phone."

"Call him back and tell him to stay back, but don't lose them. Does he have one of those walkie-talkies I bought?"

"I think so."

"If he does, tell him to call me on Channel 1 if they start for the bridge." When we started our surveillance, I purchased the newest military type walkie-talkies.

"What if they are coming to the Club?"

"I'm going to Nina. After I leave, send Bill home and you wait to hear from George. I'll take a walkie-talkie. Call me if they come here. I may be out of range, but try anyway."

I drove to the bridge and crossed over, parking at the visitors' center. Ten minutes later, I heard "Robert, come in, this is George."

"Go ahead George." I said, fumbling with the radio.

"They are starting on the bridge."

"Where are you?"

"I'm at the toll booth behind them. How about you?"

"I'm leaving the visitors center on my way to Captiva. I'm going to take Nina someplace safe and then go to the house."

"What should I do?"

"What do you have with you?"

"A forty four." He said, meaning his.44 caliber magnum pistol.

"Come over and see if you can pick them up. If you do, stay back, but be ready to come in. And, call me if they stop."

"Roger that."

When I reached Chico's, I figured I had five minutes or less. Racing into the store, I learned Nina had gone to lunch early. Driving directly to my house. I ran to the back door, only to find the house was still locked. Nina was walking somewhere. She could be out on the beach or walking back to the house from the village. Running back to my car, I drove down the street and parked at a neighbor's house. From the glove box, I took out the Walther I kept in the car and loaded a clip.

"George, any sign?" I called.

"They are five cars ahead of me. We have just crossed over to Captiva. Are you secure?"

"Negative. The bait is out of the trap."

"That isn't good. What do you want me to do?"

"Stay with them. And call me if they stop or come down my streets." I got out of my truck and with the Walther in my pocket.

This wasn't what I expected to happen. We expected Andy and Boca to make a move, but I assumed I could keep Nina safe. Stupid.

"Robert, come in."

"Yes," I said, grabbing the radio.

"They have parked across the street from the Bubble Room. They are going in, over."

"Into the Bubble Room?"

"Right, should I follow?"

"No, that may be what they want. Maybe they know they have a tail. Leave them, go down the street and find a place to park, and then come to my house from the front. Call me when you are in a good place.

"Roger that. Wait."

"What?"

"I see Nina; she is at the Island store crossing the street headed this way."

"Stay there, and see what she does."

"I hate to say this, but it looks like she is meeting Andy."

"Has she gone in?"

"She just did. Do you think it is an accident?"

"Do you?"

"No, it looks like another meet."

"Okay, park somewhere close, but out of sight, I'm coming to you." I drove down to the Bubble Room and parked right next to George's car. When I got out of my truck, George was at my side, with his hand in his right pocket.

"This wasn't in the plan Boss," said George smiling.

"No, the question is do we go in or wait."

"My squad leader said you should always take it to them."

"How did that work for him?"

"He's dead."

"That is what I thought, still, it is awful hot out here and I would really like to see how friendly this meeting is, wouldn't you."

"I would except there are too many rooms in there to effectively take the fight to them, I say we wait and watch. They aren't going to do anything to her in there. I think we should get out of sight and let the play unfold," said George, dragging me away.

We made it as far as Georges' car when Esteban Boca walked out and scanned the parking lot. Next, Nina walked out, followed by Andy Valdez. Nina showed no sign of affection, but on the other hand, she wasn't afraid. Crouching behind the car's bumper, I almost missed Frank Valdez. Frank was followed by two other men, Andy's bodyguards, Heckle and Jeckle.

"The whole gang whispered George."

Frank Valdez said something to Heckle and he ran off, presumably to get a car. While they waited, Frank talked with Andy and Nina. When the car arrived, Jeckle ran to the car and opened the door for Frank, who stepped up to Nina and offered her his hand. Leaning in she kissed his cheek instead. In the next instance, Frank was in the car and gone, leaving Nina, Andy, and Boca on the corner.

Andy said something to Boca, who ran to another car, leaving Andy and Nina alone. Standing in the sun, neither spoke or touched until the car arrived. Checking left and right, Andy handed Nina a package.

"Drugs," said George.

"Or a gun."

"Do we brace her?"

"No, let's see what she does and what happens to the package."

Shading her eyes to the sun, Nina looked around and then walked home. Following in our cars, I parked in the driveway and George parked behind. Nina was still in the kitchen with the package on the counter when we entered my house.

"A gift from Don Valdez?" I said. Nina made for the package, but I grabbed her arm as George grabbed the package and on a nod from me opened it." Placing the wrapping paper on the counter, George held up a plastic baggie half filled with white power and a .25 caliber Heckler & Koch HK4 pistol. A gun even smaller than my Walther.

"So Nina, what is this?"

"Two days ago, Frank Valdez, called the house. He said he was calling for me. He said Andy was sorry for all the trouble he had caused. Frank said Andy wanted to meet and personally apologize. He said he would be at the meetings to ensure nothing happened. So I agreed."

"You agreed but didn't tell me."

"You wouldn't have let me go."

"No, probably not, but why not tell me?"

158

"What, so you would be in the Bubble Room to greet Andy."

"Tell me about the baggy and the .25."

"Andy gave the package to me after his uncle left. I don't think Frank knew. All he said was just in case."

"Just in case you needed a fix or a gun?"

"It was a joke."

"Not a very funny one."

"What did the Frank say during your meeting?"

"He told me that Andy and Esteban would never bother me again. He said so long as you and I stay out of his business and out of Immokalee, we had nothing to fear."

"Anything else?"

"He said, George should spend more time in the store and less time driving around in the Everglades. Do you know what that means?"

"Yeah, it means George was observed watching Andy."

"You have been watching Andy."

"Yes."

"Were you watching me too?"

"Sometimes."

"So you lied to Frank Valdez?"

No, I did exactly as we agreed. I followed the letter of the law. I left Andy alone and I stayed out of Immokalee."

"Frank may not see it that way. You said you would stay out of his business, but now it turns out you have been following Andy."

"So?"

"So what if Frank considers your agreement void?"

"I don't know, actually. I'm still thinking about the dope and the gun. Look, I've got to be honest. If you have agreed to kill me for Don Valdez or for Andy's sake, I wish you would do it now. I hate living a lie."

"Robert, how can you talk to me like that? I'm here with you. I met with Don Valdez, because he asked and one doesn't turn down a man like Frank Valdez. At lunch, he was completely reasonable. He said he had spoken to Andy and his crew and I had his word no one in his family would ever bother me again. "

"That sounds like he is weaseling. No one in his family. I wish he had said no one in his employment."

"Well, I believe him, and Andy was a nice as he could be. He said he was sorry all the trouble he had caused. He apologized and kissed my hand."

"What about Boca?"

"Esteban sat at another table. He had nothing to say!"

"Okay, before we let down our guard, I suggest we have the contents of this bag examined," I said taking the baggie.

"And the gun," said George, taking the .25 cal.

George took the gun apart at the kitchen table while I made a few calls.

"The gun is clean. It works properly, the firing pin is good. Short of the checking the rounds, I'd say it is a great carry piece."

"Okay, let's take one of the bullets apart just to be sure they aren't loaded with C4 or something exotic." I went to a drawer in the

160

kitchen and grabbed two sets of pliers. With a little effort, I pulled the bullet out of the shell and poured out the contents. Everything looked normal, but to be on the safe side, I pulled apart all the shells and then dumped the contents in the trash outside.

"What now?" asked Nina.

"I called Saul. He has a friend coming over to test the stuff."

Saul's friend turned out to be a twenty-year chemistry student at South Florida Community. He took the baggie, opened a backpack, removed some bottle of chemicals and proceeded to test the contents.

"Very fine stuff," he said. "Too good, really."

"What do you mean, too good?"

"This is heroin mixed with cocaine, a speedball. Dangerous, especially if you didn't know what it was. If you thought this was cocaine."

"What did he tell you this was, I asked?"

"He said it was H."

"Did you ask him to fix you up?"

"Of course not."

"Would this speedball kill a user?"

"It could, a new user perhaps."

"Do you want it?"

"No, I'm just a chemist."

"Okay, I'm going to dump it in the ocean. Any objections?" Nina was silent. I left with the baggie. When I returned I gave Saul's friend fifty bucks for his trouble, and he left.

Nina said she needed air, and left George and me to sit on the front porch. I made ice tea in a pitcher. When I got out three glasses, George said he thought he should go.

On the porch, Nina was crying.

"Nina," I began, but did not know what to say. Frank and Andy had put a wedge between us.

"Robert, I know you care for me. The question is when are you going to trust me? When will you believe I know what I'm doing?" I wanted to trust Nina, but the needle kit from Andy remained in her suitcase, and her suitcase remained packed. From one day to the next, I never knew if Nina would be there when I came home.

"I want to," I said, "but you should have told me about this meeting."

"Frank asked me not to tell you."

"Yes, and Andy gave you a package. What did he tell you to do?"

"He didn't say anything."

"Of course he did, I saw him."

"He said he had Boca cut a special speedball for me. I used to love Speedballs. He said if I wanted more, all I had to do was to put a bullet in your head. He said if I did that, I could come back." She started crying again.

"Did he say anything else?"

"He said he loved me."

DEFENSIVE POSITIONS
Chapter 10

The Marines and the Special Forces believe in taking the battle to the enemy. They teach that waiting, taking a defensive position, never wins a war, it only delays it. Of course, there are many famous examples where that philosophy has proven disastrous, for example, Gettysburg. With Nina locked in the guest room crying, I didn't feel ready to take anything to Andy and his crew, so I recruited some help, I called Jack Jenson.

When Jack came on the phone, I explained that Nina was staying with me for a while, and I mentioned my understanding with Frank and his recent lunch meeting with Nina. I did not see any reason to mention Andy's package. Rather, I asked if Jack had seen Tom Burton.

"Tom came around just the other day. He asked about Nina. He said he had been ready to fly to Detroit when someone named Cabot called and left word she was safe but in hiding in Florida. My guess is Tom is waiting to see if she turns up in Immokalee."

"Well, I don't think he should learn she is here with me on Captiva quite yet. What do you think he would do if he knew where Andy was picking up drug deliveries?"

"My guess is the police already know and do nothing. What's being unloaded?"

"Marijuana I think."

"I know several people who might pay for that information."

"It is my gift to you," I said, describing the two drop off spots and the times when we had observed the drop offs. When I finished, I debated saying more, but I didn't want to be directly involved, so I said. "Good talking to you," and left it at that.

In the days that followed, I divided my time between Nina and the Club. In the morning, Nina and I walked to work. Some days I'd come home early and walked her home and we'd make dinner together. On the days when I was at the Club late, Nina would have a meal waiting. On Sunday, we slept in and watched TV or went to a movie. Sometimes we had sex, but most of the time we simply slept together. Whatever happened, I always felt it was Nina who was in control.

For the most part, we avoided any conversation about Andy, Esteban, or Frank Valdez. For a crime boss, I allowed that Frank was an honorable man, but in my opinion, Andy and Boca could not be trusted. I knew from these conversations that Nina wanted to see Andy, moreover, what got me was how often Nina talked as if Andy was completely innocent and even defended Boca.

On one occasion, I tried to make it clear that Andy was a bad man. "He is engaged in criminal activity." I said, stating the obvious. "Eventually he will be killed or go to jail. If you are with Andy, you will certainly take up drugs again, and end up dead or in prison.

"One day he will break free of his uncle," she declared.

"One day he hopes to be his uncle. The problem is he isn't smart enough or man enough."

"He might not be as smart as you, but at least he loves me. You do not love me. You can't even say the words." What she said was true. I guess. I'm not sure I've ever loved anyone, except Saul and George, and Joe Kaminski. With Nina. I wanted to protect her. I wanted to save her from Ardy. Most of all, I wanted her to become someone I could trust, but right now, I didn't and she knew it.

On Sunday, there was an article in the Ft. Myers Daily News reported the police were investigating a plane crash for evidence of a drug drop gone badly. According to the report, a bullet riddled Piper Cub had been found a mile off Oil Well road on the way to the Cork Screw Bird Sanctuary. Detective Tom Burton of the Immokalee police had found the plane. Burton speculated that the plane was a part of a failed drug deal. The report said the plane was registered to a businessman in Columbia and had been reported stolen a day before it was discovered in Florida.

I called Saul and told him about the bust. I asked him to watch out for Bill and he promised he would. Two weeks later, Detective Burton was mentioned as part of a drug enforcement team who caught another plane on the ground when it landed with two bales of marijuana. According to the report, the police exchanged fire with men in a truck waiting for the plane and arrested the pilot of the plane, a citizen of Mexico. Given the street value of marijuana, the papers estimated the police had confiscated a minimum of one hundred and twenty thousand dollars' worth of marijuana. A day later, I called Jack Jenson.

"The shit has really hit the fan here," said Jensen. "Wherever I go I see guys in gray suits and dark glassed.

"FBI?"

"Could be the FBI, or Columbians."

"Any news about the Don."

"I heard he is in Bogota."

"What about Tom Burton?"

"Tom is getting a lot of credit in the local papers. I saw him yesterday. He was walking on Main Street. He reminded me of that guy in Walking Tall."

"The guy with the baseball bat."

"Right. Just asking for it. Anybody could have taken him out."

"Does he know about Nina?"

"Not from me. He asked, though."

"What did you tell him?"

"I said as far as I knew she was clean, safe, and happy."

"I'm not so sure about the last part."

"What's wrong?"

"She thinks I don't trust her and she's right. She misses Immokalee and Andy. If something happens to Andy she is going to blame me."

"The way things are going, something is sure to happen to Andy or Tom. Nothing to do with you. Least not any more. Those two boys have been on a collision course, since they met in high school."

"I'm sure Nina knows that, but she also knows I had been following Andy. Looking for a way to take him out."

"You know, Robert, trust between a man and a woman is a funny thing. Not always the same as trust between men."

"What do you mean?"

"Men trust one another when they can depend on each other. A man can lie to another man about all kinds of things, but if he has his back, they have trust. With women, it is different. If a man lies or cheats on his woman, she may take him back, but she will never trust him."

"What are you saying?"

"Tell Nina everything. Tell her that you gave me information, but that you have had no hand in what is happening. Convince her what you did was because you care for her. Show her she can trust you and that you trust her."

"That's the problem. I'm not sure I do trust her."

"Has she lied to you?"

"Not really."

"Then you have everything a man can expect from a woman."

"Thanks, I think."

"Good talking to you. And, watch yourself."

"You too."

That night I told Nina that I had given Jack Jenson the location of the two drug drops. I told her, my guess was the tribe had stolen the first shipment, and Jack had given Tom the information for the second. I told her I was doing this for her. That I was trying to stop Andy without having to kill him or get Tom killed.

"What do you care?" Nina asked.

"I don't really. Andy Valdez is a criminal, but Tom is a decent guy."

"Why are you as telling me this?"

"I don't want there to be secrets between us. I'm being honest because I care about you."

"Robert, you are only fooling yourself. If you really cared about me, you wouldn't be trying to get Andy and Tom to kill each other. Somehow, you think if you don't pull the trigger you are not to blame. However, you have put the ball in motion and now you are doing what you do best."

"What is that?"

"You're watching and waiting."

When she finished, I didn't feel any better and she didn't seem any closer, but at least I had not lied to her and she did not leave.

The news that Frank Valdez had been gunned down at the airport in Bogota, Columbia was all over the radio the next morning. Jack Jenson called me from his home. He said he got a call from one of the local newspaper reporters. The reporter said one of Frank's nephews and a bodyguard had been killed also.

Hearing that Frank Valdez had been killed truly saddened me, but knowing that Andy was no longer, a problem gave me some

168

relief. An hour later, the news update said that Frank and his nephew Stephen and a man named Chico Hernandez had been shot by three-masked gunman as they were entering a car at the airport. The gunmen escaped.

I had an entirely different reaction to the story when I learned that Andy was not the nephew killed. It was it possible Andy had set up his Uncle. Then it hit me that Andy would be the head of the Valdez family and once he was, how long would I remain alive.

Calling in Saul, George, and Bill, we discussed our options before I called Jack Jensor at the bar. It was eleven thirty in the afternoon on Friday, but no one answered. Worried, I called Chico's only to learn Nina had gone home early.

"I think we should close up." I said to Bill, Saul, and George. "Bill, I'd like you to come home with me. George and Saul, you do what makes the most sense. Both of you are welcome to stay on Captiva until we know what is shaking.

"I better go home. Sandy is waiting. I will be okay."

"I think I will go with George, but you may see me later. Either way I will call."

"What about tomorrow?" asked George. He was scheduled to open the club.

"Unless you hear from me, open the Club as usual. Just be careful. Wear a vest. If Andy is going to take over the family business he isn't going to start a local war."

"I'm not sure," said Saul. "If he is directly involved in his Uncles' murder, he will want to get rid of every enemy as quickly as possible. There could be contracts on Jack and Tom, and all of us. If the Lieutenants accept him as Don he has the resources to kill everyone tonight."

"All the more reason to get somewhere secure and wait. I'm going home. Call me there when you are safe. And, make sure you carry some extra supplies home with you." We all went to our gun lockers and then to the ammo supplies. Bill had been practicing with a .38 caliber police special, so I grabbed a rental gun from the case. Along with two boxes of bullets. Next, I put a Winchester pump and shells in a carry bag, along with an M10 sub machine gun. Finally, I added a Colt .45, and three vests. I knew all this was over doing it and would be pointless if they had already gotten to Nina, but I felt better when Bill and I were armed and on the road.

Pulling into my drive, the house looked normal. Telling Bill to wait in the car with his .38 ready, I opened the trunk, put on a vest, put the Walther in the holster, and carried the M10 at my side. From the drive, I could see the back door was open. Walking around to the front of the house, I found Nina in the yard. She's changed from her work clothes to shorts and a tee shirt. She looked beautiful. Seeing me wearing my vest with a gun at my side, she started. For a moment, it seemed like she might run.

"What is it? Why are you home? What happened?" she demanded.

"Frank Valdez is dead. Murdered in Columbia this morning. One of Andy's brothers, Stephen was with him. I called Jack's, to find out what is happening in Immokalee, but there was no answer at the bar.

"That isn't possible, Jack is always there."

"I know. If it wasn't for you and Bill, I'd go there."

"To Immokalee?"

I'm worried Andy will try to clean house. The smart move is to take out his competition along with any other heirs."

"There's only his younger brother and Esteban."

"What do you mean Esteban?"

"Esteban is Andy's cousin."

"Maybe Esteban is the one spreading his wings," I said.

"Esteban wouldn't do this. He loved the Don."

"What about Andy?"

"Andy was always jealous of the Don, but, he could never kill him."

"Maybe not, but what about hiring someone in Columbia?"

"He might do that!"

"Then it's possible he will send someone after you. I think we should go in," I said, looking down the beach. "What's for dinner?"

"I bought chicken and coleslaw. I thought we'd barbeque."

"Is there enough for Bill?"

"I think so."

"What if Saul shows up?"

"Definitely not."

"Okay, I'm going to try Jack again, and then I'll run to the Island store."

"Remember, they close at seven."

I called Jack's from the kitchen phone. After five rings, a man answered "Hello."

"Is Jack there?"

"No, the bar is closed."

"I need to talk to Jack. It's very important."

"Mr. Jenson is dead. This is Officer Juarez. Who is this?"

"Robert Cederberg. What happened?"

"Mister Jenson was shot in the bar."

"What about Detective Tom Burton? Does he know Jack has been shot? He needs to know."

"Detective Burton was here, but he has gone. Who is this again?"

"My name is Cederberg, I've reason to believe Andy Valdez or Esteban Boca was involved in killing Mister Jenson."

"No, we have his killer."

"Who is it?"

"I'm not at liberty to say."

"How did you catch his killer, so fast?"

"I really can't talk about the case."

"Office Juarez. Whoever killed Jack may come after me. Please tell me what happened," I pleaded. It took a moment before he answered.

"Mister Jenson was alone when was attacked. His killer walked in and shot him three times. He was behind the bar. The man left without robbing the till."

"So it was a hit."

"Yes, but none of the shots were immediately fatal. Jenson got to the front door and shot the man twice with a shotgun before he expired."

"Can you tell me if the killer worked for Frank Valdez?"

"I'm sorry I cannot confirm or deny anything."

"Okay. If you see Tom Burton, tell him it is critical that he call me at this number."

I gave him my name and number and made him repeat it. Before going down stairs, I called Saul and he said he was coming over. Nina immediately broke down and ran to her room crying when I gave her the news.

Feeling there was little I could do to help Nina, I decided to walk to the Island store for supplies before they closed. Handing Bill a loaded .38 I went out the front and walk down the beach to the Mucky Duck.

The Duck was crowded with the sunset crowd and beach walkers in to toast the day. Scanning the crowd, I saw no one I knew and nothing out of the ordinary. The Island store is at the end of Andy Rosse Lane. Anticipating Saul's appetite, I bought another chicken, two six packs of beer, several bags of chips, along with cookies for Bill. On my way back, I stopped at the Duck to watch the sun set. The noisy crowd let out a loud cheer when the sun dropped below the water, creating a momentary flare of green. According to the tour guides, the end of a perfect day.

At the front door, I called to Bill before stepping up to the porch door. When he did not answer, I pulled out my Walther and opened the front door. Nothing happened; the alarm was off. From the living room, I saw Bill on the kitchen floor in a pool of blood. The back door was open. Looking out the back, I saw my truck was gone. Calling out to Nina there was no response. Bill was unconscious but breathing. He had a large bleeding gash on his head and beside him on the floor was the .38 revolver.

I got a towel from the bath and held it against the wound on Bill's head. I knew it would need stitches, so I called the police and asked if they would send a car and an ambulance. When I said my name, the dispatcher said she already had the address. After that, I again checked for Nina, but I knew she was gone.

Bill was conscious by the time that the police arrive, most of the bleeding had stopped and he was able to explain what happened.

"You left and Nina seemed fine, then I said I was sorry about Jack, and she started crying and ran into the bedroom. When she came out, she went to watch at the back door. The last thing I remember, she called me to the kitchen, and someone decked me," said Bill.

"Was it Nina," I asked.

"Maybe. Funny thing is she said she was sorry and kissed me on the head, before running out the back door. I had the impression a small dark featured man stood over me, and then followed her out," he added.

I left a note for Saul asking him to come to the Sanibel hospital and then went in the ambulance with Bill. On the way, Bill took my arm and said, "I don't understand."

"I don't either, but I'm going to get some answers."

Saul showed up while Bill's head was being stitched.

We talked about Nina and Jack Jenson while we drank weak coffee in the emergency room waiting area. What worried me most was the thought that Esteban had been in my house again.

The ER doctor came out to inform us he wanted to keep Bill overnight. At my house, Saul cleaned the kitchen floor while I called George. When he learned about Nina and Esteban, he asked whether I thought Esteban force her to leave or was he simply there to help her escape?

"I'm afraid I've been a fool," I admitted to Saul after getting off the phone with George. We sat at the kitchen table with a bottle of tequila and limes.

"Robert, Nina is a beautiful girl, and I like her. I really do, but who can tell with a girl like her. She was a junkie who supported her habit by selling her body. Her whole life was a lie. You offered her a new life, but maybe it wasn't enough. I'm thinking that meeting with Andy wasn't saying goodbye, she was reconnecting. Perhaps you are better off with her gone."

"I suppose you are right. Let her go back to Andy. Good riddance. The problem is someone nearly killed Bill. Attacking my family requires a response."

"Now wait a minute Robert. If Boca was at your house again, Nina probably saved Bill." Saul rubbed his jaw for effect. All he will have is a bump and a few stitches. I say leave the Valdez family and come back the Club.

"I'd like to, the only thing is what happens when Andy and Boca learn I was responsible for his family losing a quarter of a million dollars in drugs.

"Yes, that could be a deal breaker, especially since you don't have any of the money."

Over shots of tequila, Saul and I decided the first order of business was making sure our families remained safe while we figured out what to do about Andy and Boca. Sitting at the kitchen table, I called Tom Burton at home to see what he knew about Jack or Nina. He answered on the fourth ring; his voice was slurred with sleep or booze. When I identified myself and asked if he knew me, he said, "You are the guy who called about Jack."

"You didn't call back."

"Why should I?"

"Because I was protecting Nina."

"Aren't you now?"

"No, I think she has gone back to Andy. What can you tell me about what happened to Jack Jenson and Frank Valdez?"

"Jack was shot in his own bar by Chico Hernandez. The little fucker walked in at eleven in the morning, pulled out a .38 and started firing. His mistake was he walked out without being sure Jack was dead. That tough old cracker let him have it with two barrels from a sawed off he kept under the bar."

"Chico. Isn't he the prizefighter who worked for Frank Valdez? Why would he go after Jack?"

"I guess you know that Frank Valdez and his nephew Stephen were gunned down in Bogota."

"I heard."

"DEA thinks Frank was in Bogotá to explain how he lost two shipments. They think the cartel was sending a message."

"How does that involve Jack Jenson?"

"The rumor here is Jack was responsible for high jacking those shipments. Word is the tribe is tired of the spicks making all the easy money. So they staged an ambush on that first shipment."

"What about the second, I thought you were there for the arrest."

"I was, I got a tip."

"From Jack?"

"I can't really say. But that bust did me a lot of good in the department and with the federal boys."

"What about Andy? What happened to him, and Boca?"

"Near as I know, Andy was home when his uncle was killed; he was meeting with the city council standing in for his uncle. When

Jack was shot, he and his mother were at the funeral parlor making arrangements."

"Ironclad alibis."

"Right, ironclad not that it matters.

"So what will happen to the family business?"

"Andy is the next oldest male in the family. With his brother Stephen gone, he is the heir apparent. There is no one to challenge him on the farm. He is twenty-three, and his younger brother is seventeen and cut from the same cloth.

"What about someone else in the drug cartel?"

"That might depend on what happens next. If Andy can take charge and effectively receive the goods and run the vendors, he could be fine. If he loses another shipment or has some other disaster, my guess is he will not have to fly to Columbia to be gunned down."

"Is that going to happen?"

"I can't really talk about these things especially over the phone."

"How about Andy's man Boca? What has happened to him?"

"No one has seen him for a while."

"Could he have been in Columbia?" I asked.

"That sounds like a good working theory. You think Andy took his Uncle out?"

"I think Boca might have. I just learned Boca is Andy's cousin. He's Frank's sisters' boy. I think it is possible Boca was here when Nina left."

"Okay, I'm nearly sober, tell me about Nina," said Tom.

I explained about Nina as best as I could. When I finished, Burton laughed and then apologized.

"She did it to you just like she did it to me. She captures you and draws you into her lies and her life with Andy and you think you are helping her. You think I can change her, but she always goes back, back to the drugs and back to that little prick Andy."

"What if Andy was out of the picture. Would she go to you?" I asked.

"I've been in love with Nina since high school. We were going to college together and then she got pregnant. She said she was on the pill, but she got pregnant. We fought. She said she was going to have an abortion. I wanted to get married and have the baby. Andy came on the scene and his Uncle Frank arranged for her to lose the baby. After that, she refused to see me, and moved in with Andy. Then she started taking drugs and fucking other guys, so Andy threw her out."

"What did she do?"

"She ran back to me. She said she wanted to get clean, so, I helped her get off the drugs. But then she started working at Jacks and as soon as she had a little money, she went right back to Andy and the drugs."

"How many times has she been in Rehab?"

179

"Four, not counting the jail time."

"So you think she was playing you and me?"

"I hate to say this, but you and Andy and I are all in the same club.

"How about Jack Jenson?" I asked.

"He might have been, but I think Jack really just wanted to watch out for her. She is part of the tribe. He claimed she was family."

"Anyone else in the Club I should worry about?"

"I'd watch Esteban."

"Nina told me he gave her the drugs that nearly killed her."

"That may be right, but her landlady said she was having this big fight."

"With Andy?"

"No, she was arguing with Esteban. The landlady said she had the impression they had sex and then they fought and he left. I think she took that speedball on her own after he was gone. For my money, Esteban is the other man."

"Jesus."

"Yes, she is a complicated woman."

"So what are you going to do?" I asked Tom.

"I'm going back to bed. Nina is back where she wants to be. You offered her the best chance for a life she has had in years and she gave it up for a drug addled prick and his murderous cousin. She is welcome to the life she gets, as short as that may be. I'm done with her. And if you'll take my advice, you should wipe your hands of her."

"Good advice," I said, knowing I wasn't going to take it.

In the morning when I went out to get my paper, my truck was in the drive with the keys under the seat. On the dashboard was a note: 'Thanks for taking care of Nina. If you want to keep your friends and family out of the hospital, stay out of Immokalee.' It was signed Esteban Boca. *Good advice*, I thought, except in three days I planned on attending Jack Jenson's funeral.

LOOSE ENDS
Chapter 11

The line of cars started at the bar and ran around the street leading into the cemetery. The funeral service was much as you would expect, filled with praise and funny stories about a local character. Jack's wife cried and his two sons, both over fifty sat stoically in the front. Behind them, the mayor and sheriff, and other local dignitaries were scattered among assorted Indians and Hells Angels. George, Saul, and I sat in the back amongst the regulars from the bar. I made Bill stay and run the counter at the Club. The last thing I wanted was Andy or Boca seeing Bill as a part of what was about to go down.

When the minister finished talking about what Jack would find in heaven, someone from the Seminole tribe got up and talked about the tribe's spiritual beliefs and his perceptions of where Jack might be. He was less optimistic about heaven. Jack's eldest son rose, to speak, about what was happening in Immokalee. His words were a harsh indictment. Finally, the Mayor spoke about the endless work Jack performed to make the town a better place to live, even if that took the form of beer and taco night on Tuesday. If the mayor expected a laugh, he didn't get one. When the service was over, we sat in the back watching the crowd of mourners leave, anxious to get to the bar.

Nina and Andy were sitting near the front on the side opposite the family. Andy was on the outside and when he stood, three men behind him stood. Boca sat next to Nina. When Andy turned and started down the aisle, he saw the three of us. A moment later Nina saw me and hesitate until Andy pushed her forward. When they passed, Andy and Nina put their heads down and walked on. When he reached our row, Esteban Boca stopped. He had on a black suit, with a black shirt and tie. Except for his silver-toed cowboy boots, he looked like Johnny Cash.

"Andy thought you would be sensible. But, I told him no, you are an entrometido, you have to interfere. I said you would not listen or take advice, and here you are."

"Jack was a friend. We had to pay our respects just like you."

"Now you have done so. Unless you want to join your friend, I suggest you skip the burial and go back to your beach." I noticed Andy had gotten in a limo. Nina was four steps behind watching Esteban.

"Esteban, can I ask you a question?" I said.

"One question before you leave."

"Does Andy know about you and Nina?" The look Esteban gave me caused me to doubt I would get to stand up. Then Saul set an M10 machine gun across his knees.

Esteban smiled and laughed. "This is not the time or place for more blood. Go home while Don Valdez is in mourning." he said.

"Don Valdez is dead," I replied, "and the cops think Andy arranged for the hit. Personally, I wonder where you were when the hit went down."

"What you suggest is very dangerous."

"Andy is a weakling who has to pay men like you to protect him. How long before he realizes you are fucking Nina?" Boca turned to look at Nina. She was still waiting.

"Let me know if you have a service for Frank, I would like to attend," I said, standing up with Saul at my side, still with the M10 pointed at Boca. "Until then I have a piece of advice for you,"

"What is that?"

"Stay off Captiva."

"Yes and you stay out of Immokalee."

~*~

Rather than finding the Valdez family's new drop site, we decided to determine what happened to the drugs after they arrived in Florida. Every day for a month, Saul, George, or I watched the Valdez farm. To be honest, George established our observation post and did twice as many shifts, because he enjoyed being a sniper again.

On this morning, it was my turn. It was early in July. I left Captiva just before four in the morning. George had found a spot where we could park off the road and walk in. While it was still dark, I found the spot George used as an observation blind, dug out his foxhole, and covered it with palmetto. Looking at the blind, I hoped even a seasoned hunter would walk by it without realizing it was man-made. Laying in the blind, I set out a bottle of water, high-powered binoculars, my spotting scope, a package of peanut butter sandwiches, a bag of m & ms, my silver Walther, and an empty plastic milk bottle for peeing. Using the scope, I began my morning surveillance of the Valdez farm.

Work begins early on a farm; the first to stir were groundskeepers and stable men. At six fifteen, trucks arrived filled with field workers. Brown men dressed in jeans and white work shirts assembled in the front circle. A tall white man, who I assumed was the foreman came out of a small house in the back and talked to the workers. As he talked, men moved to different trucks. Eventually all the men had loaded back in the trucks along with the foreman and the trucks drove off.

Boca arrive at nine in the morning driving a new Dodge pickup truck. Getting out of his truck, he grabbed a black jacket from the passenger seat. Putting on the jacket, I could see a he was wearing a shoulder holster. While Boca struggled to get his coat over the gun, Andy walked out the house with a cup of coffee in one hand and Nina at his side. Andy had on tan slacks, black shirt, and a jacket similar to Bocas.

Nina looked haggard, as if she hadn't slept. Her eyes looked dark, almost sunken. Kissing Nina goodbye, Andy left with Boca. For two hours, nothing much happened, workers came and then Andy and Boca returned around one driving the truck straight into the main barn. Minutes later a dozen men arrived in a truck. These men wore white pants and shirts. I assumed they were drug processors.

As each man entered the barn, Boca standing by the door made a check on a clipboard. After several minutes, Andy walked across to the yard to the farmhouse leaving Boca to supervise the workers. Two hours later a line of cars and trucks arrived, each vehicle with two occupants. Waiting in turn, each pulled up to the barn, the passenger got out, spent five minutes or less, and then the car drove off. The whole operation took three hours from delivery to distribution. I spent another hour observing before I crawled out from the blind and back to my truck.

It took several weeks of observation before a pattern seemed to emerge. Using the calendar, the first shipment we observed was on a Tuesday, followed by another delivery on Wednesday of the same week. Nothing happened for a week, and then new deliveries occurred on Friday and Saturday. Apparently, the two busts had caused the family to change their delivery schedule. As near as we could tell, two new drug shipments came in every week plus a day. To check on our predictions, we skipped five days and then observed the next five days. As predicted, a shipment arrived on Friday and Saturday. After observing two more deliveries, I knew we were ready.

I called Detective Sergeant Hill in Naples and told him I had a lead on where the Valdez drug shipments were arriving and how they were distributed. I called Hill because he wasn't on the Drug enforcement team and he was from Naples. Most important, I trusted him and I knew his bosses put a lot of faith in his information and leadership. From a law enforcement perspective, catching the drugs when they land meant a new airplane for the police department. On the other hand, the men at the drop off were gophers. Expendables. Waiting until the shipment was at the farm meant capturing the main players. The distributors and the dealers. For Hill the decision was easy, catching a dozen dealers along with several kilos of cocaine or marijuana was pure political gold, particularly for an honest Hispanic cop. The problem was trusting the Feds and the Police and Sheriff's departments in Immokalee.

In September, Detective Sergeant Hill watched the entire transaction on a Monday and again on Tuesday. When he was convinced, he called Tom Burton. The next deliveries were expected on Thursday and Friday of the following week. Walking to our cars, Hill asked me where I would be next Friday and I said I wasn't sure. He told me to be somewhere public and safe, with lots of witnesses. I said I would be someplace safe. What I didn't tell Sergeant Hill was I planned to be sitting right where we were, watching the whole thing from our lookout post above the Valdez farm.

I was dressing when George and Saul showed up at three a.m. with pistols and donuts. I hadn't asked either to come along, but when I told George I wasn't coming in I guess he and Sal put two and three together.

"Is there time to make coffee?" asked Saul handing me a donut.

"Pour a cup of cold coffee from yesterday, we have to go. We need to be in place before the shipment or the police arrive." I said, feeling pleased at having George and Saul along.

We parked the truck in our usual spot and marched in from the south. In September, the corn was ready to harvest, but the path between rows made it easy going. Each of us carried a duffle bag.

Among the three of us, we had sufficient weapons to throw over a small Latin American government. When we reached George's observation post, George pulled out his rifle scope while Saul and I shared binoculars. It was seven in the morning, and the field workers were long gone. As usual, Boca arrived in his truck. This morning Boca was dressed like any other ranch hand, jeans and a dark work shirt. Standing on the porch, he scanned the horizon. For a long moment he covered his eyes and seemed to focus on our general vicinity. Eventually, Andy joined Boca on the porch and the two men talked until Andy went back inside leaving Boca on the porch.

At ten, a truck arrived with five men and drove into barn followed by the lab workers. The shipment was early and it had not picked up by Andy or Boca. They had changed the pattern on the very day a bust was planned. Two hours later, the first dealer arrived and Boca started giving orders. I had to consider the possibility that Andy and Boca had an informant in one of the departments, and knew about the planned bust.

Soon, cars and trucks packed the yard and the first dealers were leaving. I hope we'd see the police to swoop in once the dealers arrived, but nothing happened and when the dealers started leaving, we started to pack up too. Just then, shots rang out from the backside of the barn and men and vehicles started flying in all directions. From our vantage spot, we watched as a row of cars raced down the front drive and officers on foot came running in from every corner of the farm. At first, it looked like the whole arrest might go down with only shots in the air, but then Boca stepped onto the porch with a

189

machine gun and started spraying the police cars charging down the front drive. The lead car took several hits before it swerved off the road. The second car turned sideways and took a full burst of in the passenger door. The driver emerged from his side, but no one got out on the passenger side. The third car was luckier; blocked by the other two the driver stopped and four officers bailed out. From the door of the car, an officer fired at the spot where Esteban had been only seconds before. Whether Andy wanted it or not, Boca had started a war.

For several minutes, all was quiet, and then more automatic fire came from several upstairs windows, drawing return fire from officers behind car doors and on the ground. Listening to the firefight, Saul said, "There were several shooters, now there is only one shooter. He is moving back and forth from the windows. He's giving someone time to escape."

All was quiet until someone on a loudspeaker called into the house and barn for everyone to walk out with their hands in the air. Initially three farm workers walked out of the barn with their hands in the air. After a second warning, several lab workers and dealers emerged from the barn. Next, an old man and an old woman came out of the house, followed by two small children. Several officers came forward with guns drawn and moved the men in one direction and the old woman and children in another. Once again, the man on the loud speaker called to the house demanding that everyone come out with their hands in the air.

Eventually, Nina came out looking like she needed a fix. She was shoeless, and wearing a robe. She looked thinner. In her arms, she carried a small dog. On the steps to the porch, she hesitated and looked back at the house. Then she staggered around until a policeman dragged her to safety. For several more minutes, the yard was quiet, then four policemen rushed the house, one going in the front door while another threw tear gas in the open front window. Two more ran around the house. From our position, we didn't see what happened, but we heard explosions and what may have been shots.

Finally, a policeman came out indicating it was safe. Soon after, number of wounded officers left in ambulances with sirens blaring. We watched for a while, but, when the first police cars left, we did too. During the entire raid, I never saw Tom Burton or Martin Hill.

Back on Captiva, we watched the six o'clock news anxious to hear about Andy and Esteban. The Ft. Myers station showed pictures of the farm from the air, followed by an interview with a 'federal' officer who explained that the police following on a tip had raided the farm of local grower Frank Valdez and found cocaine and marijuana along with dozen of illegal firearms. According to the reporter, three police officers were wounded, one who was in serious condition.

Hearing this news, I called Tom Burton at the police station in Immokalee. After some persuasion, the officer on the phone gave me over to the Desk Sergeant who eventually informed me that officer Burton had been killed in the line of duty. According to the Sergeant, Office Burton was shot by a man in the house who was later found dead in a secret room. He had taken his own life. I described Andy and Esteban Boca. According to the officer, the man could have been Andy Valdez, but they were waiting for positive identification. From what he said, Boca was not among those arrested. When I asked about Sergeant Hill, I learn he was one of the officers in the hospital. This news threw me. The fact that we didn't see Hill during the bust, didn't really register with me until then. My plan was for Martin Hill to bust Andy Valdez and Esteban Boca, thus ensuring they would spend twenty years in jail. Now my only friend among the police was in the hospital and Esteban Boca was on the lamb and somewhere in all of this, Nina Grace was once again a loose end.

Saul, George, and I talked for a while about we should do next. George announced he was opening the Bullseye tomorrow as usual, and then went home to be with his wife. I called Bill in Naples and told him what was happening. Knowing the easiest way to get at me was through Bill, I asked him to go stay with George for a few days. Naturally, Bill objected, but when I explained about Boca he agreed.

At dusk, Saul and I walked around the perimeter of my house, adding a new set of trip wires. We ran the wires into an existing panel in the kitchen. If someone broke the wire a light would go off on the panel. When we finished, we sat in the kitchen playing gin rummy. On the table were four loaded pistols, extra clips, and

192

two shotguns. If Esteban came at us, we were prepared. After midnight, I took the first watch while Saul slept on the couch. Around three we switched.

When Saul shook me awake, it was pitch black out the upstairs window. "We have visitors," he whispered.

"Where?" I asked, picking up the Walther off the coffee table.

"Someone tripped the wire in the front yard." We had placed several trip wires in the front and back. The beach wire in front had been tripped.

Waiting for an attack is never easy. In this case, we watched the little panel of lights. First the front yard light went off, then the side, then the backyard. Our intruder was circling the house. Next the light indicating someone was standing on the back steps came on. Signaling to Saul to set up a cross fire, I moved to the kitchen and stood behind the back door.

I saw the doorknob move, someone testing the door. Crouching I expected a man to bust the door in, instead someone knocked, and then called out, "Robert." It was Nina.

I moved to the door. "What are you doing here?" I called out.

"The police raided the farm. I was arrested, but they let me go. I hitched hiked here because I didn't have anywhere else."

"You still don't."

"Robert, Andy's dead. The police killed him." I could hear her crying.

"What are you talking about," I said slowly opening the door. Nina stood on the top back step. She had on jeans and a T-shirt that said 'Immokalee.' In her right hand, she had a clutch purse. Behind her was nothing but darkness.

"Please let me in. Andy's dead and I have nowhere to go."

"Stay right there. You made your choice when you went back to Andy and the drugs."

"But, he's dead and I need your help."

"I gave you everything I had to offer, I have nothing more," I said.

"All you offered was a glass box. You gave me nothing of yourself," she cried.

"So you went back to Andy and a life of drugs."

"I thought I was in love with Andy. However, he'd changed. All he talked about was the money he owed the Columbians."

"What about Boca?"

"It's different with Esteban." Her voice changed its tone.

"Where is Esteban?"

"I don't know, he got away."

"Tell me about Andy."

"Please let me in!"

"Explain first."

"Andy told me he and Esteban were going out through the back tunnel. They needed time. Esteban went out on the porch and fired at the cops. I did the same from inside the house except I fired into the air. I just wanted to give them a chance to escape.

194

"What tunnel?"

"There is a panel in the downstairs bedroom that opens to a tunnel Uncle Frank had built. They called it the fire tunnel. It led into the back cornfield. I thought they were both going out that way, but I guess Andy went in the safe room."

"What safe room?"

"Frank had a safe room. It's in the study. Andy and I use to go there to get it on. When the police went in the house, they found Andy in the safe room and killed him. "

"Are you sure the police shot Andy, because they didn't mention him on the news."

"After I came out, the police went in and I heard shots."

"Was Esteban still in the house when you walked out?"

"No, I don't think so!"

"How can you be sure he wasn't cleaning up loose ends?" Nina gave me a funny look, hesitated, and then looked behind her.

"Where is Esteban now? Is he out there somewhere in the dark? One last loose end to clean up. Is that what he told you? What about you? First Frank, then Andy, and now me and you. Did he give you a gun? Is there a gun in your purse? What's the first thing I taught you? Did you check to see if it was loaded?" She looked down at the purse.

"The police killed Andy."

"Bullshit. I talked to one of the Sergeants on the scene. He said Andy was dead when they found him. They said his death looked like a suicide, but you and I know Andy wouldn't kill himself.

He went to the safe room to hide. Boca shot Andy and left the gun in Andy's hand. Then he escaped out the tunnel. My guess is he brought you here or he told you to come here and he would get you later."

She started to cry. I noticed the little light for the front step come on the panel in the kitchen. Someone was on the steps to the screened porch. Looking at the front door, I saw Saul looking at Nina. Pulling a second gun from my waistband, I pointed the gun at the front door. My action refocused Saul.

Boca came crashing halfway through the front door, firing a machine gun through the opening. In the same instance, Nina stepped into the kitchen with a pistol in her hand. Saul, behind the couch, unloaded his gun at Boca, and I did the same from the kitchen. As our first bullets raced toward Boca, his tore across the living room stitching across the kitchen counter and cupboards. In the exchange, Nina dropped to her knees. Dropping the gun, she called out "Esteban," but he was on the floor.

Standing, she staggered out the back door.

Knowing Nina wasn't a threat, I used a napkin to pick up her gun and moved to the living room to check on Saul. Saul stood over Esteban with one of the colts in his hand. Esteban was crawling towards the front door; his dropped machine gun was just out of reach. From the exit wounds and blood on his back, I guessed he had taken several bullets in his chest and one in the leg.

"Saul," I said. "I am going after Nina. Will you take care of Esteban? He gave this to Nina." I handed Saul Nina's .25 automatic. My guess is it is empty, but you should check."

"Take your time," said Saul cocking the .25. "I'll call the police."

On the back steps, there was a tail of blood leading to the beach. I followed the trail of blood and Nina's at a distance still careful that someone wasn't waiting in ambush. In the moonlight, I saw Nina walking slowly with labored steps towards the ocean. At the water's edge, she stopped and looked back at me. Perhaps she thought about all she had lost, or just how lost she was. Whatever her thoughts, she started into the water wading out until she could swim. Standing at the water's edge, all I could think about was that first night I saw her. Perhaps I should have left her alone. You can never tell what will happen when you start tilting at windmills. In the distance, a small caliber shot rang out and Nina started swimming to Texas. I wished her luck.

ABOUT THE AUTHOR

Roger Lubeck lives in California and divides his time between writing, publishing, photography, and business consulting. He is President of **Corporate Behavior Analysts, Ltd**., a California based leadership and management consulting firm and Roger is President/Publisher of **It Is What It Is Press**. Roger has over 30 years consulting in real estate services, healthcare, higher education, manufacturing, and mental health. Roger is the author of a number of publications on customer service, leadership, management, marketing, and sales.

Roger and Chris Hanson are the authors of:

- *Finding the Right Path: A Guide to Leading and Managing a Title Insurance Company*, 2011.

- *Finding the Right Strategy: How to Grow Income in a Title Insurance Company, 2014*

Roger has a degree in Experimental Psychology from Utah State University and M.A. and B.S. degrees in Behavioral Psychology from Western Michigan University. In his career, Roger has been a business consultant, workshop leader, retreat facilitator, public speaker, speechwriter, assistant professor, researcher, parent trainer, and dogcatcher. Roger is married to Lynette Chandler. Lynette is an Emeritus Professor in the Northern Illinois University Department of Special Education. She is an author and national authority on Early Childhood Special Education.

Roger has published five novels including:

- *To the Western Border: A Fantasy Adventure*, 2011.

- *Bullseye,* the first Robert Cederberg novel, 2011.

- *Captiva*, the second Robert Cederberg novel, 2012.

- *Port Royal*, the third Robert Cederberg novel, 2013.

- *Key West*, the fourth Robert Cederberg novel, 2015

Roger was the Editor/Publisher on:

- *The Day Before the End of the World*, by the Journey, 2012

- *Stories from Other Worlds*, by the Writing Journey, 2014.

- *Every Book Counts: The Stories of My Life*, by Samuel C. Chandler, 2015.

- *Voices from the Dark*, by The Writing Journey, 2015.

IT IS WHAT IT IS PRESS

Roger C. Lubeck, To the Western Border: A Fantasy Adventure, Cloverdale, CA, It Is What It Is Press, 2011.

Roger C. Lubeck, Bullseye, Cloverdale, CA, It Is What It Is Press, 2011

Roger C. Lubeck, Captiva, Cloverdale, CA, It Is What It Is Press, 2012.

Roger C. Lubeck, Port Royal, Cloverdale, CA, It Is What It Is Press, 2013.

Roger C. Lubeck, Key West, Cloverdale, CA, It Is What It Is Press, 2015.

The Journey, The Day Before the End of the World, ed. Roger C. Lubeck, Cloverdale, CA, It Is What It Is Press, 2012.

The Writing Journey, Stories from Other Worlds, ed. Ana Koulouris and Roger C. Lubeck, Cloverdale, CA, It Is What It Is Press, 2014.

Samuel C. Chandler, Every Book Counts: The Stories of My Life, ed. Roger C. Lubeck, Lynette Chandler, Ruth Chandler, Marianne Chandler Paredes, Cloverdale, CA, It Is What It Is Press, 2015.

The Writing Journey, Voices from the Dark, ed. Roger C. Lubeck, Phoenix Autumn, Ana Koulouris, Sara Marschand, K. C. Swier, Cloverdale, CA, It Is What It Is Press, 2015.

www.ingramcontent.com/pod-product-compliance
Lightning Source LLC
Chambersburg PA
CBHW061153170626
46809CB00003B/1081